HERETICS

by

G. K. Chesterton

"To My Father"

The Author

Gilbert Keith Chesterton was born in London, England on the 29th of May, 1874. Though he considered himself a mere "rollicking journalist," he was actually a prolific and gifted writer in virtually every area of literature. A man of strong opinions and enormously talented at defending them, his exuberant personality nevertheless allowed him to maintain warm friendships with people—such as George Bernard Shaw and H. G. Wells—with whom he vehemently disagreed.

Chesterton had no difficulty standing up for what he believed. He was one of the few journalists to oppose the Boer War. His 1922 "Eugenics and Other Evils" attacked what was at that time the most progressive of all ideas, the idea that the human race could and should breed a superior version of itself. In the Nazi experience, history demonstrated the wisdom of his once "reactionary" views.

His poetry runs the gamut from the comic 1908 "On Running After One's Hat" to dark and serious ballads. During the dark days of 1940, when Britain stood virtually alone against the armed might of Nazi Germany, these lines from his 1911 Ballad of the White Horse were often quoted:

> I tell you naught for your comfort,
> Yea, naught for your desire,
> Save that the sky grows darker yet
> And the sea rises higher.

Though not written for a scholarly audience, his biographies of authors and historical figures like Charles Dickens and St. Francis of Assisi often contain brilliant insights into their subjects. His Father Brown mystery stories, written between 1911 and 1936, are still being read and adapted for television.

His politics fitted with his deep distrust of concentrated wealth and power of any sort. Along with his friend Hilaire Belloc and in books like the 1910 "What's Wrong with the World" he advocated a view called "Distributionism" that was best summed up by his expression that every man ought to be allowed to own "three acres and a cow." Though not known as a political thinker, his political influence has circled the world. Some see in him the father of the "small is beautiful" movement and a newspaper article by him is credited with provoking Gandhi to seek a "genuine" nationalism for India rather than one that imitated the British.

Heretics belongs to yet another area of literature at which Chesterton excelled. A fun-loving and gregarious man, he was nevertheless troubled in his adolescence by thoughts of suicide. In Christianity he found the answers to the dilemmas and paradoxes he saw in life. Other books in that same series include his 1908 Orthodoxy (written in response to attacks on this book) and his 1925 The Everlasting Man. Orthodoxy is also available as electronic text.

Chesterton died on the 14th of June, 1936 in Beaconsfield, Buckinghamshire, England. During his life he published 69 books and at least another ten based on his writings have been published after his death. Many of those books are still in print. Ignatius Press is systematically publishing his collected writings.

Table of Contents

I. Introductory Remarks on the Importance of Orthodoxy

Nothing more strangely indicates an enormous and silent evil of modern society than the extraordinary use which is made nowadays of the word "orthodox." In former days the heretic was proud of not being a heretic. It was the kingdoms of the world and the police and the judges who were heretics. He was orthodox. He had no pride in having rebelled against them; they had rebelled against him. The armies with their cruel security, the kings with their cold faces, the decorous processes of State, the reasonable processes of law—all these like sheep had gone astray. The man was proud of being orthodox, was proud of being right. If he stood alone in a howling wilderness he was more than a man; he was a church. He was the centre of the universe; it was round him that the stars swung. All the tortures torn out of forgotten hells could not make him admit that he was heretical. But a few modern phrases have made him boast of it. He says, with a conscious laugh, "I suppose I am very heretical," and looks round for applause. The word "heresy" not only means no longer being wrong; it practically means being clear-headed and courageous. The word "orthodoxy" not only no longer means being right; it practically means being wrong. All this can mean one thing, and one thing only. It means that people care less for whether they are philosophically right. For obviously a man ought to confess himself crazy before he confesses himself heretical. The Bohemian, with a red tie, ought to pique himself on his orthodoxy. The dynamiter, laying a bomb, ought to feel that, whatever else he is, at least he is orthodox.

It is foolish, generally speaking, for a philosopher to set fire to another philosopher in Smithfield Market because they do not agree in their theory of the universe. That was done very frequently in the last decadence of the Middle Ages, and it failed altogether in its object. But there is one thing that is infinitely more absurd and unpractical than burning a man for his philosophy. This is the habit of saying that his philosophy does not matter, and this is done universally in the twentieth century, in the decadence of the great revolutionary period. General theories are everywhere contemned; the doctrine of the Rights of Man is dismissed with the doctrine of the Fall of Man. Atheism itself is too theological for us to-day. Revolution itself is too much of a system; liberty itself is too much of a restraint. We will have no generalizations. Mr. Bernard Shaw has put the view in a perfect epigram: "The golden rule is that there is no golden rule." We are more and more to discuss details in art, politics, literature. A man's opinion on tramcars matters; his opinion on Botticelli matters; his opinion on all things does not matter. He may turn over and explore a million objects, but he must not find that strange object, the universe; for if he does he will have a religion, and be lost. Everything matters—except everything.

Examples are scarcely needed of this total levity on the subject of cosmic philosophy. Examples are scarcely needed to show that, whatever else we think of as affecting practical affairs, we do not think it matters whether a man is a pessimist or an optimist, a Cartesian or a Hegelian, a materialist or a spiritualist. Let me, however, take a random instance. At any innocent tea-table we may easily hear a man say, "Life is not worth living." We regard it as we regard the statement that it is a fine day; nobody thinks that it can possibly have any serious effect on the man or on the world. And yet if that utterance were really believed, the world would stand on its head. Murderers would be given medals for saving men from life; firemen would be denounced for keeping men from death; poisons would be used as medicines; doctors would be called in when people were well; the Royal Humane Society would be rooted out like a horde of assassins. Yet we never speculate as to whether the conversational pessimist will strengthen or disorganize society; for we are convinced that theories do not matter.

This was certainly not the idea of those who introduced our freedom. When the old Liberals removed the gags from all the heresies, their idea was that religious and philosophical discoveries might thus be made. Their view was that cosmic truth was so important that every one ought to bear independent testimony. The modern idea is that cosmic truth is so unimportant that it cannot matter what any one says. The former freed inquiry as men loose a noble hound; the latter frees inquiry as men fling back into the sea a fish unfit for eating. Never has there been so little discussion about the nature of men as now, when, for the first time, any one can discuss it. The old restriction meant that only the orthodox were allowed to discuss religion. Modern liberty means that nobody is allowed to discuss it. Good taste, the last and vilest of human superstitions, has succeeded in silencing us where all the rest have failed. Sixty years ago it was bad taste to be an avowed atheist. Then came the Bradlaughites, the last religious men, the last men who cared about God; but they could not alter it. It is still bad taste to be an avowed atheist. But their agony has achieved just this—that now it is equally bad taste to be an avowed Christian. Emancipation has only locked the saint in the same tower of silence as the heresiarch. Then we talk about Lord Anglesey and the weather, and call it the complete liberty of all the creeds.

But there are some people, nevertheless—and I am one of them—who think that the most practical and important thing about a man is still his view of the universe. We think that for a landlady considering a lodger, it is important to know his income, but still more important to know his philosophy. We think that for a general about to fight an enemy, it is important to know the enemy's numbers, but still more important to know the enemy's philosophy. We think the question is not whether the theory of the cosmos affects matters, but whether in the long run, anything else affects them. In the fifteenth century men cross-examined and tormented a man because he preached some immoral attitude; in the nineteenth century we feted and flattered Oscar Wilde because he preached such an attitude, and then broke his heart in penal servitude because he carried it out. It may be a question which of the two methods was the more cruel; there can be no kind of question which was the more ludicrous. The age of the Inquisition has not at least the disgrace of having produced a society which made an idol of the very same man for preaching the very same things which it made him a convict for practising.

Now, in our time, philosophy or religion, our theory, that is, about ultimate things, has been driven out, more or less simultaneously, from two fields which it used to occupy. General ideals used to dominate literature. They have been driven out by the cry of "art for art's sake." General ideals used to dominate politics. They have been driven out by the cry of "efficiency," which may roughly be translated as "politics for politics' sake." Persistently for the last twenty years the ideals of order or liberty have dwindled in our books; the ambitions of wit and eloquence have dwindled in our parliaments. Literature has purposely become less political; politics have purposely become less literary. General theories of the relation of things have thus been extruded from both; and we are in a position to ask, "What have we gained or lost by this extrusion? Is literature better, is politics better, for having discarded the moralist and the philosopher?"

When everything about a people is for the time growing weak and ineffective, it begins to talk about efficiency. So it is that when a man's body is a wreck he begins, for the first time, to talk about health. Vigorous organisms talk not about their processes, but about their aims. There cannot be any better proof of the physical efficiency of a man than that he talks cheerfully of a journey to the end of the world. And there cannot be any better proof of the practical efficiency of a nation than that it talks constantly of a journey to the end of the world, a journey to the Judgment Day and the New Jerusalem. There can be no stronger sign of a coarse material health than the tendency to run after high and wild ideals; it is in the first exuberance of infancy that we cry for the moon. None of the strong men in the strong ages would have understood what you meant by working for efficiency. Hildebrand would have said that he was working not for efficiency, but for the Catholic Church. Danton would have said that he was working not for efficiency, but for liberty, equality, and fraternity. Even if the ideal of such men were simply the ideal of kicking a man downstairs, they thought of the end like men, not of the process like paralytics. They did not say, "Efficiently elevating my right leg, using, you will notice, the muscles of the thigh and calf, which are in excellent order, I—" Their feeling was quite different. They were so filled with the beautiful vision of the man lying flat at the foot of the staircase that in that ecstasy the rest followed in a flash. In practice, the habit of generalizing and idealizing did not by any means mean worldly weakness. The time of big theories was the time of big results. In the era of sentiment and fine words, at the end of the eighteenth century, men were really robust and effective. The sentimentalists conquered Napoleon. The cynics could not catch De Wet. A hundred years ago our affairs for good or evil were wielded triumphantly by rhetoricians. Now our affairs are hopelessly muddled by strong, silent men. And just as this repudiation of big words and big visions has brought forth a race of small men in politics, so it has brought forth a race of small men in the arts. Our modern politicians claim the colossal license of Caesar and the Superman, claim that they are too practical to be pure and too patriotic to be moral; but the upshot of it all is that a mediocrity is Chancellor of the Exchequer. Our new artistic philosophers call for the same moral license, for a freedom to wreck heaven and earth with their energy; but the upshot of it all is that a mediocrity is Poet Laureate. I do not say that there are no stronger men than these; but will any one say that there are any men stronger than those men of old who were dominated by their philosophy and steeped in their religion? Whether bondage be better than freedom may be discussed. But that their bondage came to more than our freedom it will be difficult for any one to deny.

The theory of the unmorality of art has established itself firmly in the strictly artistic classes. They are free to produce anything they like. They are free to write a "Paradise Lost" in which Satan shall conquer God. They are free to write a "Divine Comedy" in which heaven shall be under the floor of hell. And what have they done? Have they produced in their universality anything grander or more beautiful than the things uttered by the fierce Ghibbeline Catholic, by the rigid Puritan schoolmaster? We know that they have produced only a few roundels. Milton does not merely beat them at his piety, he beats them at their own irreverence. In all their little books of verse you will not find a finer defiance of God than Satan's. Nor will you find the grandeur of paganism felt as that fiery Christian felt it who described Faranata lifting his head as in disdain of hell. And the reason is very obvious. Blasphemy is an artistic effect, because blasphemy depends upon a philosophical conviction. Blasphemy depends upon belief and is fading with it. If any one doubts this, let him sit down seriously and try to think blasphemous thoughts about Thor. I think his family will find him at the end of the day in a state of some exhaustion.

Neither in the world of politics nor that of literature, then, has the rejection of general theories proved a success. It may be that there have been many moonstruck and misleading ideals that have from time to time perplexed mankind. But assuredly there has been no ideal in practice so moonstruck and misleading as the ideal of practicality. Nothing has lost so many opportunities as the opportunism of Lord Rosebery. He is, indeed, a standing symbol of this epoch—the man who is theoretically a practical man, and practically more unpractical than any theorist. Nothing in this universe is so unwise as that kind of worship of worldly wisdom. A man who is perpetually thinking of whether this race or that race is strong, of whether this cause or that cause is promising, is the man who will never believe in anything long enough to make it succeed. The opportunist politician is like a man who should abandon billiards because he was beaten at billiards, and abandon golf because he was beaten at golf. There is nothing which is so weak for working purposes as this enormous importance attached to immediate victory. There is nothing that fails like success.

And having discovered that opportunism does fail, I have been induced to look at it more largely, and in consequence to see that it must fail. I perceive that it is far more practical to begin at the beginning and discuss theories. I see that the men who killed each other about the orthodoxy of the Homoousion were far more sensible than the people who are quarrelling about the Education Act. For the Christian dogmatists were trying to establish a reign of holiness, and trying to get defined, first of all, what was really holy. But our modern educationists are trying to bring about a religious liberty without attempting to settle what is religion or what is liberty. If the old priests forced a statement on mankind, at least they previously took some trouble to make it lucid. It has been left for the modern mobs of Anglicans and Nonconformists to persecute for a doctrine without even stating it.

For these reasons, and for many more, I for one have come to believe in going back to fundamentals. Such is the general idea of this book. I wish to deal with my most distinguished contemporaries, not personally or in a merely literary manner, but in relation to the real body of doctrine which they teach. I am not concerned with Mr. Rudyard Kipling as a vivid artist or a vigorous personality; I am concerned with him as a Heretic—that is to say, a man whose view of things has the hardihood to differ from mine. I am not concerned with Mr. Bernard Shaw as one of the most brilliant and one of the most honest men alive; I am concerned with him as a Heretic—that is to say, a man whose philosophy is quite solid, quite coherent, and quite wrong. I revert to the doctrinal methods of the thirteenth century, inspired by the general hope of getting something done.

Suppose that a great commotion arises in the street about something, let us say a lamp-post, which many influential persons desire to pull down. A grey-clad monk, who is the spirit of the Middle Ages, is approached upon the matter, and begins to say, in the arid manner of the Schoolmen, "Let us first of all consider, my brethren, the value of Light. If Light be in itself good—" At this point he is somewhat excusably knocked down. All the people make a rush for the lamp-post, the lamp-post is down in ten minutes, and they go about congratulating each other on their unmediaeval practicality. But as things go on they do not work out so easily. Some people have pulled the lamp-post down because they wanted the electric light; some because they wanted old iron; some because they wanted darkness, because their deeds were evil. Some thought it not enough of a lamp-post, some too much; some acted because they wanted to smash municipal machinery; some because they wanted to smash something. And there is war in the night, no man knowing whom he strikes. So, gradually and inevitably, to-day, to-morrow, or the next day, there comes back the conviction that the monk was right after all, and that all depends on what is the philosophy of Light. Only what we might have discussed under the gas-lamp, we now must discuss in the dark.

II. On the negative spirit

Much has been said, and said truly, of the monkish morbidity, of the hysteria which as often gone with the visions of hermits or nuns. But let us never forget that this visionary religion is, in one sense, necessarily more wholesome than our modern and reasonable morality. It is more wholesome for this reason, that it can contemplate the idea of success or triumph in the hopeless fight towards the ethical ideal, in what Stevenson called, with his usual startling felicity, "the lost fight of virtue." A modern morality, on the other hand, can only point with absolute conviction to the horrors that follow breaches of law; its only certainty is a certainty of ill. It can only point to imperfection. It has no perfection to point to. But the monk meditating upon Christ or Buddha has in his mind an image of perfect health, a thing of clear colours and clean air. He may contemplate this ideal wholeness and happiness far more than he ought; he may contemplate it to the neglect of exclusion of essential THINGS; he may contemplate it until he has become a dreamer or a driveller; but still it is wholeness and happiness that he is contemplating. He may even go mad; but he is going mad for the love of sanity. But the modern student of ethics, even if he remains sane, remains sane from an insane dread of insanity.

The anchorite rolling on the stones in a frenzy of submission is a healthier person fundamentally than many a sober man in a silk hat who is walking down Cheapside. For many such are good only through a withering knowledge of evil. I am not at this moment claiming for the devotee anything more than this primary advantage, that though he may be making himself personally weak and miserable, he is still fixing his thoughts largely on gigantic strength and happiness, on a strength that has no limits, and a happiness that has no end. Doubtless there are other objections which can be urged without unreason against the influence of gods and visions in morality, whether in the cell or street. But this advantage the mystic morality must always have—it is always jollier. A young man may keep himself from vice by continually thinking of disease. He may keep himself from it also by continually thinking of the Virgin Mary. There may be question about which method is the more reasonable, or even about which is the more efficient. But surely there can be no question about which is the more wholesome.

I remember a pamphlet by that able and sincere secularist, Mr. G. W. Foote, which contained a phrase sharply symbolizing and dividing these two methods. The pamphlet was called BEER AND BIBLE, those two very noble things, all the nobler for a conjunction which Mr. Foote, in his stern old Puritan way, seemed to think sardonic, but which I confess to thinking appropriate and charming. I have not the work by me, but I remember that Mr. Foote dismissed very contemptuously any attempts to deal with the problem of strong drink by religious offices or intercessions, and said that a picture of a drunkard's liver would be more efficacious in the matter of temperance than any prayer or praise. In that picturesque expression, it seems to me, is perfectly embodied the incurable morbidity of modern ethics. In that temple the lights are low, the crowds kneel, the solemn anthems are uplifted. But that upon the altar to which all men kneel is no longer the perfect flesh, the body and substance of the perfect man; it is still flesh, but it is diseased. It is the drunkard's liver of the New Testament that is marred for us, which we take in remembrance of him.

Now, it is this great gap in modern ethics, the absence of vivid pictures of purity and spiritual triumph, which lies at the back of the real objection felt by so many sane men to the realistic literature of the nineteenth century. If any ordinary man ever said that he was horrified by the subjects discussed in Ibsen or Maupassant, or by the plain language in which they are spoken of, that ordinary man was lying. The average conversation of average men throughout the whole of modern civilization in every class or trade is such as Zola would never dream of printing. Nor is the habit of writing thus of these things a new habit. On the contrary, it is the Victorian prudery and silence which is new still, though it is already dying. The tradition of calling a spade a spade starts very early in our literature and comes down very late. But the truth is that the ordinary honest man, whatever vague account he may have given of his feelings, was not either disgusted or even annoyed at the candour of the moderns. What disgusted him, and very justly, was not the presence of a clear realism, but the absence of a clear idealism. Strong and genuine religious sentiment has never had any objection to realism; on the contrary, religion was the realistic thing, the brutal thing, the thing that called names. This is the great difference between some recent developments of Nonconformity and the great Puritanism of the seventeenth century. It was the whole point of the Puritans that they cared nothing for decency. Modern Nonconformist newspapers distinguish themselves by suppressing precisely those nouns and adjectives which the founders of Nonconformity distinguished themselves by flinging at kings and queens. But if it was a chief claim of religion that it spoke plainly about evil, it was the chief claim of all that it spoke plainly about good. The thing which is resented, and, as I think, rightly resented, in that great modern literature of which Ibsen is typical, is that while the eye that can perceive what are the wrong things increases in an uncanny and devouring clarity, the eye which sees what things are right is growing mistier and mistier every moment, till it goes almost blind with doubt. If we compare, let us say, the morality of the DIVINE COMEDY with the morality of Ibsen's GHOSTS, we shall see all that modern ethics have really done. No one, I imagine, will accuse the author of the INFERNO of an Early Victorian prudishness or a Podsnapian optimism. But Dante describes three moral instruments—Heaven, Purgatory, and Hell, the vision of perfection, the vision of improvement, and the vision of failure. Ibsen has only one—Hell. It is often said, and with perfect truth, that no one could read a play like GHOSTS and remain indifferent to the necessity of an ethical self-command. That is quite true, and the same is to be said of the most monstrous and material descriptions of the eternal fire. It is quite certain the realists like Zola do in one sense promote morality—they promote it in the sense in which the hangman promotes it, in the sense in which the devil promotes it. But they only affect that small minority which will accept any virtue of courage. Most healthy people dismiss these moral dangers as they dismiss the possibility of bombs or microbes. Modern realists are indeed Terrorists, like the dynamiters; and they fail just as much in their effort to create a thrill. Both realists and dynamiters are well-meaning people engaged in the task, so obviously ultimately hopeless, of using science to promote morality.

I do not wish the reader to confuse me for a moment with those vague persons who imagine that Ibsen is what they call a pessimist. There are plenty of wholesome people in Ibsen, plenty of good people, plenty of happy people, plenty of examples of men acting wisely and things ending well. That is not my meaning. My meaning is that Ibsen has throughout, and does not disguise, a certain vagueness and a changing attitude as well as a doubting attitude towards what is really wisdom and virtue in this life—a vagueness which contrasts very remarkably with the decisiveness with which he pounces on something which he perceives to be a root of evil, some convention, some deception, some ignorance. We know that the hero of GHOSTS is mad, and we know why he is mad. We do also know that Dr. Stockman is sane; but we do not know why he is sane. Ibsen does not profess to know how virtue and happiness are brought about, in the sense that he professes to know how our modern sexual tragedies are brought about. Falsehood works ruin in THE PILLARS OF SOCIETY, but truth works equal ruin in THE WILD DUCK. There are no cardinal virtues of Ibsenism. There is no ideal man of Ibsen. All this is not only admitted, but vaunted in the most valuable and thoughtful of all the eulogies upon Ibsen, Mr.

Bernard Shaw's QUINTESSENCE OF IBSENISM. Mr. Shaw sums up Ibsen's teaching in the phrase, "The golden rule is that there is no golden rule." In his eyes this absence of an enduring and positive ideal, this absence of a permanent key to virtue, is the one great Ibsen merit. I am not discussing now with any fullness whether this is so or not. All I venture to point out, with an increased firmness, is that this omission, good or bad, does leave us face to face with the problem of a human consciousness filled with very definite images of evil, and with no definite image of good. To us light must be henceforward the dark thing—the thing of which we cannot speak. To us, as to Milton's devils in Pandemonium, it is darkness that is visible. The human race, according to religion, fell once, and in falling gained knowledge of good and of evil. Now we have fallen a second time, and only the knowledge of evil remains to us.

A great silent collapse, an enormous unspoken disappointment, has in our time fallen on our Northern civilization. All previous ages have sweated and been crucified in an attempt to realize what is really the right life, what was really the good man. A definite part of the modern world has come beyond question to the conclusion that there is no answer to these questions, that the most that we can do is to set up a few notice-boards at places of obvious danger, to warn men, for instance, against drinking themselves to death, or ignoring the mere existence of their neighbours. Ibsen is the first to return from the baffled hunt to bring us the tidings of great failure.

Every one of the popular modern phrases and ideals is a dodge in order to shirk the problem of what is good. We are fond of talking about "liberty"; that, as we talk of it, is a dodge to avoid discussing what is good. We are fond of talking about "progress"; that is a dodge to avoid discussing what is good. We are fond of talking about "education"; that is a dodge to avoid discussing what is good. The modern man says, "Let us leave all these arbitrary standards and embrace liberty." This is, logically rendered, "Let us not decide what is good, but let it be considered good not to decide it." He says, "Away with your old moral formulae; I am for progress." This, logically stated, means, "Let us not settle what is good; but let us settle whether we are getting more of it." He says, "Neither in religion nor morality, my friend, lie the hopes of the race, but in education." This, clearly expressed, means, "We cannot decide what is good, but let us give it to our children."

Mr. H.G. Wells, that exceedingly clear-sighted man, has pointed out in a recent work that this has happened in connection with economic questions. The old economists, he says, made generalizations, and they were (in Mr. Wells's view) mostly wrong. But the new economists, he says, seem to have lost the power of making any generalizations at all. And they cover this incapacity with a general claim to be, in specific cases, regarded as "experts", a claim "proper enough in a hairdresser or a fashionable physician, but indecent in a philosopher or a man of science." But in spite of the refreshing rationality with which Mr. Wells has indicated this, it must also be said that he himself has fallen into the same enormous modern error. In the opening pages of that excellent book MANKIND IN THE MAKING, he dismisses the ideals of art, religion, abstract morality, and the rest, and says that he is going to consider men in their chief function, the function of parenthood. He is going to discuss life as a "tissue of births." He is not going to ask what will produce satisfactory saints or satisfactory heroes, but what will produce satisfactory fathers and mothers. The whole is set forward so sensibly that it is a few moments at least before the reader realises that it is another example of unconscious shirking. What is the good of begetting a man until we have settled what is the good of being a man? You are merely handing on to him a problem you dare not settle yourself. It is as if a man were asked, "What is the use of a hammer?" and answered, "To make hammers"; and when asked, "And of those hammers, what is the use?" answered, "To make hammers again". Just as such a man would be perpetually putting off the question of the ultimate use of carpentry, so Mr. Wells and all the rest of us are by these phrases successfully putting off the question of the ultimate value of the human life.

The case of the general talk of "progress" is, indeed, an extreme one. As enunciated today, "progress" is simply a comparative of which we have not settled the superlative. We meet every ideal of religion, patriotism, beauty, or brute pleasure with the alternative ideal of progress—that is to say, we meet every proposal of getting something that we know about, with an alternative proposal of getting a great deal more of nobody knows what. Progress, properly understood, has, indeed, a most dignified and legitimate meaning. But as used in opposition to precise moral ideals, it is ludicrous. So far from it being the truth that the ideal of progress is to be set against that of ethical or religious finality, the reverse is the truth. Nobody has any business to use the word "progress" unless he has a definite creed and a cast-iron code of morals. Nobody can be progressive without being doctrinal; I might almost say that nobody can be progressive without being infallible—at any rate, without believing in some infallibility. For progress by its very name indicates a direction; and the moment we are in the least doubtful about the direction, we become in the same degree doubtful about the progress. Never perhaps since the beginning of the world has there been an age that had less right to use the word "progress" than we. In the Catholic twelfth century, in the philosophic eighteenth century, the direction may have been a good or a bad one, men may have differed more or less about how far they went, and in what direction, but about the direction they did in the main agree, and consequently they had the genuine sensation of progress. But it is precisely about the direction that we disagree. Whether the future excellence lies in more law or less law, in more liberty or less liberty; whether property will be finally concentrated or finally cut up; whether sexual passion will reach its sanest in an almost virgin intellectualism or in a full animal freedom; whether we should love everybody with Tolstoy, or spare nobody with Nietzsche;—these are the things about which we are actually fighting most. It is not merely true that the age which has settled least what is progress is this "progressive" age. It is, moreover, true that the people who have settled least what is progress are the most "progressive" people in it. The ordinary mass, the men who have never troubled about progress, might be trusted perhaps to progress. The particular individuals who talk about progress would certainly fly to the four winds of heaven when the pistol-shot started the race. I do not, therefore, say that the word "progress" is unmeaning; I say it is unmeaning without the previous definition of a moral doctrine, and that it can only be applied to groups of persons who hold that doctrine in common. Progress is not an illegitimate word, but it is logically evident that it is illegitimate for us. It is a sacred word, a word which could only rightly be used by rigid believers and in the ages of faith.

III. On Mr. Rudyard Kipling and Making the World Small

There is no such thing on earth as an uninteresting subject; the only thing that can exist is an uninterested person. Nothing is more keenly required than a defence of bores. When Byron divided humanity into the bores and bored, he omitted to notice that the higher qualities exist entirely in the bores, the lower qualities in the bored, among whom he counted himself. The bore, by his starry enthusiasm, his solemn happiness, may, in some sense, have proved himself poetical. The bored has certainly proved himself prosaic.

We might, no doubt, find it a nuisance to count all the blades of grass or all the leaves of the trees; but this would not be because of our boldness or gaiety, but because of our lack of boldness and gaiety. The bore would go onward, bold and gay, and find the blades of grass as splendid as the swords of an army. The bore is stronger and more joyous than we are; he is a demigod—nay, he is a god. For it is the gods who do not tire of the iteration of things; to them the nightfall is always new, and the last rose as red as the first.

The sense that everything is poetical is a thing solid and absolute; it is not a mere matter of phraseology or persuasion. It is not merely true, it is ascertainable. Men may be challenged to deny it; men may be challenged to mention anything that is not a matter of poetry. I remember a long time ago a sensible sub-editor coming up to me with a book in his hand, called "Mr. Smith," or "The Smith Family," or some such thing. He said, "Well, you won't get any of your damned mysticism out of this," or words to that effect. I am happy to say that I undeceived him; but the victory was too obvious and easy. In most cases the name is unpoetical, although the fact is poetical. In the case of Smith, the name is so poetical that it must be an arduous and heroic matter for the man to live up to it. The name of Smith is the name of the one trade that even kings respected, it could claim half the glory of that arma virumque which all epics acclaimed. The spirit of the smithy is so close to the spirit of song that it has mixed in a million poems, and every blacksmith is a harmonious blacksmith.

Even the village children feel that in some dim way the smith is poetic, as the grocer and the cobbler are not poetic, when they feast on the dancing sparks and deafening blows in the cavern of that creative violence. The brute repose of Nature, the passionate cunning of man, the strongest of earthly metals, the wierdest of earthly elements, the unconquerable iron subdued by its only conqueror, the wheel and the ploughshare, the sword and the steam-hammer, the arraying of armies and the whole legend of arms, all these things are written, briefly indeed, but quite legibly, on the visiting-card of Mr. Smith. Yet our novelists call their hero "Aylmer Valence," which means nothing, or "Vernon Raymond," which means nothing, when it is in their power to give him this sacred name of Smith—this name made of iron and flame. It would be very natural if a certain hauteur, a certain carriage of the head, a certain curl of the lip, distinguished every one whose name is Smith. Perhaps it does; I trust so. Whoever else are parvenus, the Smiths are not parvenus. From the darkest dawn of history this clan has gone forth to battle; its trophies are on every hand; its name is everywhere; it is older than the nations, and its sign is the Hammer of Thor. But as I also remarked, it is not quite the usual case. It is common enough that common things should be poetical; it is not so common that common names should be poetical. In most cases it is the name that is the obstacle. A great many people talk as if this claim of ours, that all things are poetical, were a mere literary ingenuity, a play on words. Precisely the contrary is true. It is the idea that some things are not poetical which is literary, which is a mere product of words. The word "signal-box" is unpoetical. But the thing signal-box is not unpoetical; it is a place where men, in an agony of vigilance, light blood-red and sea-green fires to keep other men from death.

That is the plain, genuine description of what it is; the prose only comes in with what it is called. The word "pillar-box" is unpoetical. But the thing pillar-box is not unpoetical; it is the place to which friends and lovers commit their messages, conscious that when they have done so they are sacred, and not to be touched, not only by others, but even (religious touch!) by themselves. That red turret is one of the last of the temples. Posting a letter and getting married are among the few things left that are entirely romantic; for to be entirely romantic a thing must be irrevocable. We think a pillar-box prosaic, because there is no rhyme to it. We think a pillar-box unpoetical, because we have never seen it in a poem. But the bold fact is entirely on the side of poetry. A signal-box is only called a signal-box; it is a house of life and death. A pillar-box is only called a pillar-box; it is a sanctuary of human words. If you think the name of "Smith" prosaic, it is not because you are practical and sensible; it is because you are too much affected with literary refinements. The name shouts poetry at you. If you think of it otherwise, it is because you are steeped and sodden with verbal reminiscences, because you remember everything in Punch or Comic Cuts about Mr. Smith being drunk or Mr. Smith being henpecked. All these things were given to you poetical. It is only by a long and elaborate process of literary effort that you have made them prosaic.

Now, the first and fairest thing to say about Rudyard Kipling is that he has borne a brilliant part in thus recovering the lost provinces of poetry. He has not been frightened by that brutal materialistic air which clings only to words; he has pierced through to the romantic, imaginative matter of the things themselves. He has perceived the significance and philosophy of steam and of slang. Steam may be, if you like, a dirty by-product of science. Slang may be, if you like, a dirty by-product of language. But at least he has been among the few who saw the divine parentage of these things, and knew that where there is smoke there is fire—that is, that wherever there is the foulest of things, there also is the purest. Above all, he has had something to say, a definite view of things to utter, and that always means that a man is fearless and faces everything. For the moment we have a view of the universe, we possess it.

Now, the message of Rudyard Kipling, that upon which he has really concentrated, is the only thing worth worrying about in him or in any other man. He has often written bad poetry, like Wordsworth. He has often said silly things, like Plato. He has often given way to mere political hysteria, like Gladstone. But no one can reasonably doubt that he means steadily and sincerely to say something, and the only serious question is, What is that which he has tried to say? Perhaps the best way of stating this fairly will be to begin with that element which has been most insisted by himself and by his opponents—I mean his interest in militarism. But when we are seeking for the real merits of a man it is unwise to go to his enemies, and much more foolish to go to himself.

Now, Mr. Kipling is certainly wrong in his worship of militarism, but his opponents are, generally speaking, quite as wrong as he. The evil of militarism is not that it shows certain men to be fierce and haughty and excessively warlike. The evil of militarism is that it shows most men to be tame and timid and excessively peaceable. The professional soldier gains more and more power as the general courage of a community declines. Thus the Pretorian guard became more and more important in Rome as Rome became more and more luxurious and feeble. The military man gains the civil power in proportion as the civilian loses the military virtues. And as it was in ancient Rome so it is in contemporary Europe. There never was a time when nations were more militarist. There never was a time when men were less brave. All ages and all epics have sung of arms and the man; but we have effected simultaneously the deterioration of the man and the fantastic perfection of the arms. Militarism demonstrated the decadence of Rome, and it demonstrates the decadence of Prussia.

And unconsciously Mr. Kipling has proved this, and proved it admirably. For in so far as his work is earnestly understood the military trade does not by any means emerge as the most important or attractive. He has not written so well about soldiers as he has about railway men or bridge builders, or even journalists. The fact is that what attracts Mr. Kipling to militarism is not the idea of courage, but the idea of discipline. There was far more courage to the square mile in the Middle Ages, when no king had a standing army, but every man had a bow or sword. But the fascination of the standing army upon Mr. Kipling is not courage, which scarcely interests him, but discipline, which is, when all is said and done, his primary theme. The modern army is not a miracle of courage; it has not enough opportunities, owing to the cowardice of everybody else. But it is really a miracle of organization, and that is the truly Kiplingite ideal. Kipling's subject is not that valour which properly belongs to war, but that interdependence and efficiency which belongs quite as much to engineers, or sailors, or mules, or railway engines. And thus it is that when he writes of engineers, or sailors, or mules, or steam-engines, he writes at his best. The real poetry, the "true romance" which Mr. Kipling has taught, is the romance of the division of labour and the discipline of all the trades. He sings the arts of peace much more accurately than the arts of war. And his main contention is vital and valuable. Every thing is military in the sense that everything depends upon obedience. There is no perfectly epicurean corner; there is no perfectly irresponsible place. Everywhere men have made the way for us with sweat and submission. We may fling ourselves into a hammock in a fit of divine carelessness. But we are glad that the net-maker did not make the hammock in a fit of divine carelessness. We may jump upon a child's rocking-horse for a joke. But we are glad that the carpenter did not leave the legs of it unglued for a joke. So far from having merely preached that a soldier cleaning his side-arm is to be adored because he is military, Kipling at his best and clearest has preached that the baker baking loaves and the tailor cutting coats is as military as anybody.

Being devoted to this multitudinous vision of duty, Mr. Kipling is naturally a cosmopolitan. He happens to find his examples in the British Empire, but almost any other empire would do as well, or, indeed, any other highly civilized country. That which he admires in the British army he would find even more apparent in the German army; that which he desires in the British police he would find flourishing, in the French police. The ideal of discipline is not the whole of life, but it is spread over the whole of the world. And the worship of it tends to confirm in Mr. Kipling a certain note of worldly wisdom, of the experience of the wanderer, which is one of the genuine charms of his best work.

The great gap in his mind is what may be roughly called the lack of patriotism—that is to say, he lacks altogether the faculty of attaching himself to any cause or community finally and tragically; for all finality must be tragic. He admires England, but he does not love her; for we admire things with reasons, but love them without reasons. He admires England because she is strong, not because she is English. There is no harshness in saying this, for, to do him justice, he avows it with his usual picturesque candour. In a very interesting poem, he says that—

"If England was what England seems"

—that is, weak and inefficient; if England were not what (as he believes) she is—that is, powerful and practical—

"How quick we'd chuck 'er! But she ain't!"

He admits, that is, that his devotion is the result of a criticism, and this is quite enough to put it in another category altogether from the patriotism of the Boers, whom he hounded down in South Africa. In speaking of the really patriotic peoples, such as the Irish, he has some difficulty in keeping a shrill irritation out of his language. The frame of mind which he really describes with beauty and nobility is the frame of mind of the cosmopolitan man who has seen men and cities.

"For to admire and for to see,
For to be'old this world so wide."

He is a perfect master of that light melancholy with which a man looks back on having been the citizen of many communities, of that light melancholy with which a man looks back on having been the lover of many women. He is the philanderer of the nations. But a man may have learnt much about women in flirtations, and still be ignorant of first love; a man may have known as many lands as Ulysses, and still be ignorant of patriotism.

Mr. Rudyard Kipling has asked in a celebrated epigram what they can know of England who know England only. It is a far deeper and sharper question to ask, "What can they know of England who know only the world?" for the world does not include England any more than it includes the Church. The moment we care for anything deeply, the world—that is, all the other miscellaneous interests—becomes our enemy. Christians showed it when they talked of keeping one's self "unspotted from the world;" but lovers talk of it just as much when they talk of the "world well lost." Astronomically speaking, I understand that England is situated on the world; similarly, I suppose that the Church was a part of the world, and even the lovers inhabitants of that orb. But they all felt a certain truth—the truth that the moment you love anything the world becomes your foe. Thus Mr. Kipling does certainly know the world; he is a man of the world, with all the narrowness that belongs to those imprisoned in that planet. He knows England as an intelligent English gentleman knows Venice. He has been to England a great many times; he has stopped there for long visits. But he does not belong to it, or to any place; and the proof of it is this, that he thinks of England as a place. The moment we are rooted in a place, the place vanishes. We live like a tree with the whole strength of the universe.

The globe-trotter lives in a smaller world than the peasant. He is always breathing, an air of locality. London is a place, to be compared to Chicago; Chicago is a place, to be compared to Timbuctoo. But Timbuctoo is not a place, since there, at least, live men who regard it as the universe, and breathe, not an air of locality, but the winds of the world. The man in the saloon steamer has seen all the races of men, and he is thinking of the things that divide men—diet, dress, decorum, rings in the nose as in Africa, or in the ears as in Europe, blue paint among the ancients, or red paint among the modern Britons. The man in the cabbage field has seen nothing at all; but he is thinking of the things that unite men—hunger and babies, and the beauty of women, and the promise or menace of the sky. Mr. Kipling, with all his merits, is the globe-trotter; he has not the patience to become part of anything. So great and genuine a man is not to be accused of a merely cynical cosmopolitanism; still, his cosmopolitanism is his weakness. That weakness is splendidly expressed in one of his finest poems, "The Sestina of the Tramp Royal," in which a man declares that he can endure anything in the way of hunger or horror, but not permanent presence in one place. In this there is certainly danger. The more dead and dry and dusty a thing is the more it travels about; dust is like this and the thistle-down and the High Commissioner in South Africa. Fertile things are somewhat heavier, like the heavy fruit trees on the pregnant mud of the Nile. In the heated idleness of youth we were all rather inclined to quarrel with the implication of that proverb which says that a rolling stone gathers no moss. We were inclined to ask, "Who wants to gather moss, except silly old ladies?" But for all that we begin to perceive that the proverb is right. The rolling stone rolls echoing from rock to rock; but the rolling stone is dead. The moss is silent because the moss is alive.

The truth is that exploration and enlargement make the world smaller. The telegraph and the steamboat make the world smaller. The telescope makes the world smaller; it is only the microscope that makes it larger. Before long the world will be cloven with a war between the telescopists and the microscopists. The first study large things and live in a small world; the second study small things and live in a large world. It is inspiriting without doubt to whizz in a motor-car round the earth, to feel Arabia as a whirl of sand or China as a flash of rice-fields. But Arabia is not a whirl of sand and China is not a flash of rice-fields. They are ancient civilizations with strange virtues buried like treasures. If we wish to understand them it must not be as tourists or inquirers, it must be with the loyalty of children and the great patience of poets. To conquer these places is to lose them. The man standing in his own kitchen-garden, with fairyland opening at the gate, is the man with large ideas. His mind creates distance; the motor-car stupidly destroys it. Moderns think of the earth as a globe, as something one can easily get round, the spirit of a schoolmistress. This is shown in the odd mistake perpetually made about Cecil Rhodes. His enemies say that he may have had large ideas, but he was a bad man. His friends say that he may have been a bad man, but he certainly had large ideas. The truth is that he was not a man essentially bad, he was a man of much geniality and many good intentions, but a man with singularly small views. There is nothing large about painting the map red; it is an innocent game for children. It is just as easy to think in continents as to think in cobble-stones. The difficulty comes in when we seek to know the substance of either of them. Rhodes' prophecies about the Boer resistance are an admirable comment on how the "large ideas" prosper when it is not a question of thinking in continents but of understanding a few two-legged men. And under all this vast illusion of the cosmopolitan planet, with its empires and its

Reuter's agency, the real life of man goes on concerned with this tree or that temple, with this harvest or that drinking-song, totally uncomprehended, totally untouched. And it watches from its splendid parochialism, possibly with a smile of amusement, motor-car civilization going its triumphant way, outstripping time, consuming space, seeing all and seeing nothing, roaring on at last to the capture of the solar system, only to find the sun cockney and the stars suburban.

IV. Mr. Bernard Shaw

In the glad old days, before the rise of modern morbidities, when genial old Ibsen filled the world with wholesome joy, and the kindly tales of the forgotten Emile Zola kept our firesides merry and pure, it used to be thought a disadvantage to be misunderstood. It may be doubted whether it is always or even generally a disadvantage. The man who is misunderstood has always this advantage over his enemies, that they do not know his weak point or his plan of campaign. They go out against a bird with nets and against a fish with arrows. There are several modern examples of this situation. Mr. Chamberlain, for instance, is a very good one. He constantly eludes or vanquishes his opponents because his real powers and deficiencies are quite different to those with which he is credited, both by friends and foes. His friends depict him as a strenuous man of action; his opponents depict him as a coarse man of business; when, as a fact, he is neither one nor the other, but an admirable romantic orator and romantic actor. He has one power which is the soul of melodrama—the power of pretending, even when backed by a huge majority, that he has his back to the wall. For all mobs are so far chivalrous that their heroes must make some show of misfortune—that sort of hypocrisy is the homage that strength pays to weakness. He talks foolishly and yet very finely about his own city that has never deserted him. He wears a flaming and fantastic flower, like a decadent minor poet. As for his bluffness and toughness and appeals to common sense, all that is, of course, simply the first trick of rhetoric. He fronts his audiences with the venerable affectation of Mark Antony—

> "I am no orator, as Brutus is;
> But as you know me all, a plain blunt man."

It is the whole difference between the aim of the orator and the aim of any other artist, such as the poet or the sculptor. The aim of the sculptor is to convince us that he is a sculptor; the aim of the orator, is to convince us that he is not an orator. Once let Mr. Chamberlain be mistaken for a practical man, and his game is won. He has only to compose a theme on empire, and people will say that these plain men say great things on great occasions. He has only to drift in the large loose notions common to all artists of the second rank, and people will say that business men have the biggest ideals after all. All his schemes have ended in smoke; he has touched nothing that he did not confuse. About his figure there is a Celtic pathos; like the Gaels in Matthew Arnold's quotation, "he went forth to battle, but he always fell." He is a mountain of proposals, a mountain of failures; but still a mountain. And a mountain is always romantic.

There is another man in the modern world who might be called the antithesis of Mr. Chamberlain in every point, who is also a standing monument of the advantage of being misunderstood. Mr. Bernard Shaw is always represented by those who disagree with him, and, I fear, also (if such exist) by those who agree with him, as a capering humorist, a dazzling acrobat, a quick-change artist. It is said that he cannot be taken seriously, that he will defend anything or attack anything, that he will do anything to startle and amuse. All this is not only untrue, but it is, glaringly, the opposite of the truth; it is as wild as to say that Dickens had not the boisterous masculinity of Jane Austen. The whole force and triumph of Mr. Bernard Shaw lie in the fact that he is a thoroughly consistent man. So far from his power consisting in jumping through hoops or standing on his head, his power consists in holding his own fortress night and day. He puts the Shaw test rapidly and rigorously to everything that happens in heaven or earth. His standard never varies. The thing which weak-minded revolutionists and weak-minded Conservatives really hate (and fear) in him, is exactly this, that his scales, such as they are, are held even, and that his law, such as it is, is justly enforced. You may attack his principles, as I do; but I do not know of any instance in which you can attack their application. If he dislikes lawlessness, he dislikes the lawlessness of Socialists as much as that of Individualists. If he dislikes the fever of patriotism, he dislikes it in Boers and Irishmen as well as in Englishmen. If he dislikes the vows and bonds of marriage, he dislikes still more the fiercer bonds and wilder vows that are made by lawless love. If he laughs at the authority of priests, he laughs louder at the pomposity of men of science. If he condemns the irresponsibility of faith, he condemns with a sane consistency the equal irresponsibility of art. He has pleased all the bohemians by saying that women are equal to men; but he has infuriated them by suggesting that men are equal to women. He is almost mechanically just; he has something of the terrible quality of a machine. The man who is really wild and whirling, the man who is really fantastic and incalculable, is not Mr. Shaw, but the average Cabinet Minister. It is Sir Michael Hicks-Beach who jumps through hoops. It is Sir Henry Fowler who stands on his head. The solid and respectable statesman of that type does really leap from position to position; he is really ready to defend anything or nothing; he is really not to be taken seriously. I know perfectly well what Mr. Bernard Shaw will be saying thirty years hence; he will be saying what he has always said. If thirty years hence I meet Mr. Shaw, a reverent being with a silver beard sweeping the earth, and say to him, "One can never, of course, make a verbal attack upon a lady," the patriarch will lift his aged hand and fell me to the earth. We know, I say, what Mr. Shaw will be, saying thirty years hence. But is there any one so darkly read in stars and oracles that he will dare to predict what Mr. Asquith will be saying thirty years hence?

The truth is, that it is quite an error to suppose that absence of definite convictions gives the mind freedom and agility. A man who believes something is ready and witty, because he has all his weapons about him. He can apply his test in an instant. The man engaged in conflict with a man like Mr. Bernard Shaw may fancy he has ten faces; similarly a man engaged against a brilliant duellist may fancy that the sword of his foe has turned to ten swords in his hand. But this is not really because the man is playing with ten swords, it is because he is aiming very straight with one. Moreover, a man with a definite belief always appears bizarre, because he does not change with the world; he has climbed into a fixed star, and the earth whizzes below him like a zoetrope. Millions of mild black-coated men call themselves sane and sensible merely because they always catch the fashionable insanity, because they are hurried into madness after madness by the maelstrom of the world.

People accuse Mr. Shaw and many much sillier persons of "proving that black is white." But they never ask whether the current colour-language is always correct. Ordinary sensible phraseology sometimes calls black white, it certainly calls yellow white and green white and reddish-brown white. We call wine "white wine" which is as yellow as a Blue-coat boy's legs. We call grapes "white grapes" which are manifestly pale green. We give to the European, whose complexion is a sort of pink drab, the horrible title of a "white man"—a picture more blood-curdling than any spectre in Poe.

Now, it is undoubtedly true that if a man asked a waiter in a restaurant for a bottle of yellow wine and some greenish-yellow grapes, the waiter would think him mad. It is undoubtedly true that if a Government official, reporting on the Europeans in Burmah, said, "There are only two thousand pinkish men here" he would be accused of cracking jokes, and kicked out of his post. But it is equally obvious that both men would have come to grief through telling the strict truth. That too truthful man in the restaurant; that too truthful man in Burmah, is Mr. Bernard Shaw. He appears eccentric and grotesque because he will not accept the general belief that white is yellow. He has based all his brilliancy and solidity upon the hackneyed, but yet forgotten, fact that truth is stranger than fiction. Truth, of course, must of necessity be stranger than fiction, for we have made fiction to suit ourselves.

So much then a reasonable appreciation will find in Mr. Shaw to be bracing and excellent. He claims to see things as they are; and some things, at any rate, he does see as they are, which the whole of our civilization does not see at all. But in Mr. Shaw's realism there is something lacking, and that thing which is lacking is serious.

Mr. Shaw's old and recognized philosophy was that powerfully presented in "The Quintessence of Ibsenism." It was, in brief, that conservative ideals were bad, not because they were conservative, but because they were ideals. Every ideal prevented men from judging justly the particular case; every moral generalization oppressed the individual; the golden rule was there was no golden rule. And the objection to this is simply that it pretends to free men, but really restrains them from doing the only thing that men want to do. What is the good of telling a community that it has every liberty except the liberty to make laws? The liberty to make laws is what constitutes a free people. And what is the good of telling a man (or a philosopher) that he has every liberty except the liberty to make generalizations. Making generalizations is what makes him a man. In short, when Mr. Shaw forbids men to have strict moral ideals, he is acting like one who should forbid them to have children. The saying that "the golden rule is that there is no golden rule," can, indeed, be simply answered by being turned round. That there is no golden rule is itself a golden rule, or rather it is much worse than a golden rule. It is an iron rule; a fetter on the first movement of a man.

But the sensation connected with Mr. Shaw in recent years has been his sudden development of the religion of the Superman. He who had to all appearance mocked at the faiths in the forgotten past discovered a new god in the unimaginable future. He who had laid all the blame on ideals set up the most impossible of all ideals, the ideal of a new creature. But the truth, nevertheless, is that any one who knows Mr. Shaw's mind adequately, and admires it properly, must have guessed all this long ago.

For the truth is that Mr. Shaw has never seen things as they really are. If he had he would have fallen on his knees before them. He has always had a secret ideal that has withered all the things of this world. He has all the time been silently comparing humanity with something that was not human, with a monster from Mars, with the Wise Man of the Stoics, with the Economic Man of the Fabians, with Julius Caesar, with Siegfried, with the Superman. Now, to have this inner and merciless standard may be a very good thing, or a very bad one, it may be excellent or unfortunate, but it is not seeing things as they are. It is not seeing things as they are to think first of a Briareus with a hundred hands, and then call every man a cripple for only having two. It is not seeing things as they are to start with a vision of Argus with his hundred eyes, and then jeer at every man with two eyes as if he had only one. And it is not seeing things as they are to imagine a demigod of infinite mental clarity, who may or may not appear in the latter days of the earth, and then to see all men as idiots. And this is what Mr. Shaw has always in some degree done. When we really see men as they are, we do not criticise, but worship; and very rightly. For a monster with mysterious eyes and miraculous thumbs, with strange dreams in his skull, and a queer tenderness for this place or that baby, is truly a wonderful and unnerving matter. It is only the quite arbitrary and priggish habit of comparison with something else which makes it possible to be at our ease in front of him. A sentiment of superiority keeps us cool and practical; the mere facts would make our knees knock under as with religious fear. It is the fact that every instant of conscious life is an unimaginable prodigy. It is the fact that every face in the street has the incredible unexpectedness of a fairy-tale. The thing which prevents a man from realizing this is not any clear-sightedness or experience, it is simply a habit of pedantic and fastidious comparisons between one thing and another. Mr. Shaw, on the practical side perhaps the most humane man alive, is in this sense inhumane. He has even been infected to some extent with the primary intellectual weakness of his new master, Nietzsche, the strange notion that the greater and stronger a man was the more he would despise other things. The greater and stronger a man is the more he would be inclined to prostrate himself before a periwinkle. That Mr. Shaw keeps a lifted head and a contemptuous face before the colossal panorama of empires and civilizations, this does not in itself convince one that he sees things as they are. I should be most effectively convinced that he did if I found him staring with religious astonishment at his own feet. "What are those two beautiful and industrious beings," I can imagine him murmuring to himself, "whom I see everywhere, serving me I know not why? What fairy godmother bade them come trotting out of elfland when I was born? What god of the borderland, what barbaric god of legs, must I propitiate with fire and wine, lest they run away with me?"

The truth is, that all genuine appreciation rests on a certain mystery of humility and almost of darkness. The man who said, "Blessed is he that expecteth nothing, for he shall not be disappointed," put the eulogy quite inadequately and even falsely. The truth "Blessed is he that expecteth nothing, for he shall be gloriously surprised." The man who expects nothing sees redder roses than common men can see, and greener grass, and a more startling sun. Blessed is he that expecteth nothing, for he shall possess the cities and the mountains; blessed is the meek, for he shall inherit the earth. Until we realize that things might not be we cannot realize that things are. Until we see the background of darkness we cannot admire the light as a single and created thing. As soon as we have seen that darkness, all light is lightening, sudden, blinding, and divine. Until we picture nonentity we underrate the victory of God, and can realize none of the trophies of His ancient war. It is one of the million wild jests of truth that we know nothing until we know nothing.

Now this is, I say deliberately, the only defect in the greatness of Mr. Shaw, the only answer to his claim to be a great man, that he is not easily pleased. He is an almost solitary exception to the general and essential maxim, that little things please great minds. And from this absence of that most uproarious of all things, humility, comes incidentally the peculiar insistence on the Superman. After belabouring a great many people for a great many years for being unprogressive, Mr. Shaw has discovered, with characteristic sense, that it is very doubtful whether any existing human being with two legs can be progressive at all. Having come to doubt whether humanity can be combined with progress, most people, easily pleased, would have elected to abandon progress and remain with humanity. Mr. Shaw, not being easily pleased, decides to throw over humanity with all its limitations and go in for progress for its own sake. If man, as we know him, is incapable of the philosophy of progress, Mr. Shaw asks, not for a new kind of philosophy, but for a new kind of man. It is rather as if a nurse had tried a rather bitter food for some years on a baby, and on discovering that it was not suitable, should not throw away the food and ask for a new food, but throw the baby out of window, and ask for a new baby. Mr. Shaw cannot understand that the thing which is valuable and lovable in our eyes is man—the old beer-drinking, creed-making, fighting, failing, sensual, respectable man. And the things that have been founded on this creature immortally remain; the things that have been founded on the fancy of the Superman have died with the dying civilizations which alone have given them birth. When Christ at a symbolic moment was establishing His great society, He chose for its corner-stone neither the brilliant Paul nor the mystic John, but a shuffler, a snob a coward—in a word, a man. And upon this rock He has built His Church, and the gates of Hell have not prevailed against it. All the empires and the kingdoms have failed, because of this inherent and continual weakness, that they were founded by strong men and upon strong men. But this one thing, the historic Christian Church, was founded on a weak man, and for that reason it is indestructible. For no chain is stronger than its weakest link.

V. Mr. H. G. Wells and the Giants

We ought to see far enough into a hypocrite to see even his sincerity. We ought to be interested in that darkest and most real part of a man in which dwell not the vices that he does not display, but the virtues that he cannot. And the more we approach the problems of human history with this keen and piercing charity, the smaller and smaller space we shall allow to pure hypocrisy of any kind. The hypocrites shall not deceive us into thinking them saints; but neither shall they deceive us into thinking them hypocrites. And an increasing number of cases will crowd into our field of inquiry, cases in which there is really no question of hypocrisy at all, cases in which people were so ingenuous that they seemed absurd, and so absurd that they seemed disingenuous.

There is one striking instance of an unfair charge of hypocrisy. It is always urged against the religious in the past, as a point of inconsistency and duplicity, that they combined a profession of almost crawling humility with a keen struggle for earthly success and considerable triumph in attaining it. It is felt as a piece of humbug, that a man should be very punctilious in calling himself a miserable sinner, and also very punctilious in calling himself King of France. But the truth is that there is no more conscious inconsistency between the humility of a Christian and the rapacity of a Christian than there is between the humility of a lover and the rapacity of a lover. The truth is that there are no things for which men will make such herculean efforts as the things of which they know they are unworthy. There never was a man in love who did not declare that, if he strained every nerve to breaking, he was going to have his desire. And there never was a man in love who did not declare also that he ought not to have it. The whole secret of the practical success of Christendom lies in the Christian humility, however imperfectly fulfilled. For with the removal of all question of merit or payment, the soul is suddenly released for incredible voyages. If we ask a sane man how much he merits, his mind shrinks instinctively and instantaneously. It is doubtful whether he merits six feet of earth. But if you ask him what he can conquer—he can conquer the stars. Thus comes the thing called Romance, a purely Christian product. A man cannot deserve adventures; he cannot earn dragons and hippogriffs. The mediaeval Europe which asserted humility gained Romance; the civilization which gained Romance has gained the habitable globe. How different the Pagan and Stoical feeling was from this has been admirably expressed in a famous quotation. Addison makes the great Stoic say—

> "'Tis not in mortals to command success;
> But we'll do more, Sempronius, we'll deserve it."

But the spirit of Romance and Christendom, the spirit which is in every lover, the spirit which has bestridden the earth with European adventure, is quite opposite. 'Tis not in mortals to deserve success. But we'll do more, Sempronius; we'll obtain it.

And this gay humility, this holding of ourselves lightly and yet ready for an infinity of unmerited triumphs, this secret is so simple that every one has supposed that it must be something quite sinister and mysterious. Humility is so practical a virtue that men think it must be a vice. Humility is so successful that it is mistaken for pride. It is mistaken for it all the more easily because it generally goes with a certain simple love of splendour which amounts to vanity. Humility will always, by preference, go clad in scarlet and gold; pride is that which refuses to let gold and scarlet impress it or please it too much. In a word, the failure of this virtue actually lies in its success; it is too successful as an investment to be believed in as a virtue. Humility is not merely too good for this world; it is too practical for this world; I had almost said it is too worldly for this world.

The instance most quoted in our day is the thing called the humility of the man of science; and certainly it is a good instance as well as a modern one. Men find it extremely difficult to believe that a man who is obviously uprooting mountains and dividing seas, tearing down temples and stretching out hands to the stars, is really a quiet old gentleman who only asks to be allowed to indulge his harmless old hobby and follow his harmless old nose. When a man splits a grain of sand and the universe is turned upside down in consequence, it is difficult to realize that to the man who did it, the splitting of the grain is the great affair, and the capsizing of the cosmos quite a small one. It is hard to enter into the feelings of a man who regards a new heaven and a new earth in the light of a by-product. But undoubtedly it was to this almost eerie innocence of the intellect that the great men of the great scientific period, which now appears to be closing, owed their enormous power and triumph. If they had brought the heavens down like a house of cards their plea was not even that they had done it on principle; their quite unanswerable plea was that they had done it by accident. Whenever there was in them the least touch of pride in what they had done, there was a good ground for attacking them; but so long as they were wholly humble, they were wholly victorious. There were possible answers to Huxley; there was no answer possible to Darwin. He was convincing because of his unconsciousness; one might almost say because of his dulness. This childlike and prosaic mind is beginning to wane in the world of science. Men of science are beginning to see themselves, as the fine phrase is, in the part; they are beginning to be proud of their humility. They are beginning to be aesthetic, like the rest of the world, beginning to spell truth with a capital T, beginning to talk of the creeds they imagine themselves to have destroyed, of the discoveries that their forbears made. Like the modern English, they are beginning to be soft about their own hardness. They are becoming conscious of their own strength—that is, they are growing weaker. But one purely modern man has emerged in the strictly modern decades who does carry into our world the clear personal simplicity of the old world of science. One man of genius we have who is an artist, but who was a man of science, and who seems to be marked above all things with this great scientific humility. I mean Mr. H. G. Wells. And in his case, as in the others above spoken of, there must be a great preliminary difficulty in convincing the ordinary person that such a virtue is predicable of such a man. Mr. Wells began his literary work with violent visions—visions of the last pangs of this planet; can it be that a man who begins with violent visions is humble? He went on to wilder and wilder stories about carving beasts into men and shooting angels like birds. Is the man who shoots angels and carves beasts into men humble? Since then he has done something bolder than either of these blasphemies; he has prophesied the political future of all men; prophesied it with aggressive authority and a ringing decision of detail. Is the prophet of the future of all men humble? It will indeed be difficult, in the present condition of current thought about such things as pride and humility, to answer the query of how a man can be humble who does such big things and such bold things. For the only answer is the answer which I gave at the beginning of this essay. It is the humble man who does the big things. It is the humble man who does the bold things. It is the humble man who has the sensational sights vouchsafed to him, and this for three obvious reasons: first, that he strains his eyes more than any other men to see them; second, that he is more overwhelmed and uplifted with them when they come; third, that he records them more exactly and sincerely and with less adulteration from his more commonplace and more conceited everyday self. Adventures are to those to whom they are most unexpected—that is, most romantic. Adventures are to the shy: in this sense adventures are to the unadventurous.

Now, this arresting, mental humility in Mr. H. G. Wells may be, like a great many other things that are vital and vivid, difficult to illustrate by examples, but if I were asked for an example of it, I should have no difficulty about which example to begin with. The most interesting thing about Mr. H. G. Wells is that he is the only one of his many brilliant contemporaries who has not stopped growing. One can lie awake at night and hear him grow. Of this growth the most evident manifestation is indeed a gradual change of opinions; but it is no mere change of opinions. It is not a perpetual leaping from one position to another like that of Mr. George Moore. It is a quite continuous advance along a quite solid road in a quite definable direction. But the chief proof that it is not a piece of fickleness and vanity is the fact that it has been upon the whole an advance from more startling opinions to more humdrum opinions. It has been even in some sense an advance from unconventional opinions to conventional opinions. This fact fixes Mr. Wells's honesty and proves him to be no poseur. Mr. Wells once held that the upper classes and the lower classes would be so much differentiated in the future that one class would eat the other. Certainly no paradoxical charlatan who had once found arguments for so startling a view would ever have deserted it except for something yet more startling. Mr. Wells has deserted it in favour of the blameless belief that both classes will be ultimately subordinated or assimilated to a sort of scientific middle class, a class of engineers. He has abandoned the sensational theory with the same honourable gravity and simplicity with which he adopted it. Then he thought it was true; now he thinks it is not true. He has come to the most dreadful conclusion a literary man can come to, the conclusion that the ordinary view is the right one. It is only the last and wildest kind of courage that can stand on a tower before ten thousand people and tell them that twice two is four.

Mr. H. G. Wells exists at present in a gay and exhilarating progress of conservativism. He is finding out more and more that conventions, though silent, are alive. As good an example as any of this humility and sanity of his may be found in his change of view on the subject of science and marriage. He once held, I believe, the opinion which some singular sociologists still hold, that human creatures could successfully be paired and bred after the manner of dogs or horses. He no longer holds that view. Not only does he no longer hold that view, but he has written about it in "Mankind in the Making" with such smashing sense and humour, that I find it difficult to believe that anybody else can hold it either. It is true that his chief objection to the proposal is that it is physically impossible, which seems to me a very slight objection, and almost negligible compared with the others. The one objection to scientific marriage which is worthy of final attention is simply that such a thing could only be imposed on unthinkable slaves and cowards. I do not know whether the scientific marriage-mongers are right (as they say) or wrong (as Mr. Wells says) in saying that medical supervision would produce strong and healthy men. I am only certain that if it did, the first act of the strong and healthy men would be to smash the medical supervision.

The mistake of all that medical talk lies in the very fact that it connects the idea of health with the idea of care. What has health to do with care? Health has to do with carelessness. In special and abnormal cases it is necessary to have care. When we are peculiarly unhealthy it may be necessary to be careful in order to be healthy. But even then we are only trying to be healthy in order to be careless. If we are doctors we are speaking to exceptionally sick men, and they ought to be told to be careful. But when we are sociologists we are addressing the normal man, we are addressing humanity. And humanity ought to be told to be recklessness itself. For all the fundamental functions of a healthy man ought emphatically to be performed with pleasure and for pleasure; they emphatically ought not to be performed with precaution or for precaution. A man ought to eat because he has a good appetite to satisfy, and emphatically not because he has a body to sustain. A man ought to take exercise not because he is too fat, but because he loves foils or horses or high mountains, and loves them for their own sake. And a man ought to marry because he has fallen in love, and emphatically not because the world requires to be populated. The food will really renovate his tissues as long as he is not thinking about his tissues. The exercise will really get him into training so long as he is thinking about something else. And the marriage will really stand some chance of producing a generous-blooded generation if it had its origin in its own natural and generous excitement. It is the first law of health that our necessities should not be accepted as necessities; they should be accepted as luxuries. Let us, then, be careful about the small things, such as a scratch or a slight illness, or anything that can be managed with care. But in the name of all sanity, let us be careless about the important things, such as marriage, or the fountain of our very life will fail.

Mr. Wells, however, is not quite clear enough of the narrower scientific outlook to see that there are some things which actually ought not to be scientific. He is still slightly affected with the great scientific fallacy; I mean the habit of beginning not with the human soul, which is the first thing a man learns about, but with some such thing as protoplasm, which is about the last. The one defect in his splendid mental equipment is that he does not sufficiently allow for the stuff or material of men. In his new Utopia he says, for instance, that a chief point of the Utopia will be a disbelief in original sin. If he had begun with the human soul—that is, if he had begun on himself—he would have found original sin almost the first thing to be believed in. He would have found, to put the matter shortly, that a permanent possibility of selfishness arises from the mere fact of having a self, and not from any accidents of education or ill-treatment. And the weakness of all Utopias is this, that they take the greatest difficulty of man and assume it to be overcome, and then give an elaborate account of the overcoming of the smaller ones. They first assume that no man will want more than his share, and then are very ingenious in explaining whether his share will be delivered by motor-car or balloon. And an even stronger example of Mr. Wells's indifference to the human psychology can be found in his cosmopolitanism, the abolition in his Utopia of all patriotic boundaries. He says in his innocent way that Utopia must be a world-state, or else people might make war on it. It does not seem to occur to him that, for a good many of us, if it were a world-state we should still make war on it to the end of the world. For if we admit that there must be varieties in art or opinion what sense is there in thinking there will not be varieties in government? The fact is very simple. Unless you are going deliberately to prevent a thing being good, you cannot prevent it being worth fighting for. It is impossible to prevent a possible conflict of civilizations, because it is impossible to prevent a possible conflict between ideals. If there were no longer our modern strife between nations, there would only be a strife between Utopias. For the highest thing does not tend to union only; the highest thing, tends also to differentiation. You can often get men to fight for the union; but you can never prevent them from fighting also for the differentiation. This variety in the highest thing is the meaning of the fierce patriotism, the fierce nationalism of the great European civilization. It is also, incidentally, the meaning of the doctrine of the Trinity.

But I think the main mistake of Mr. Wells's philosophy is a somewhat deeper one, one that he expresses in a very entertaining manner in the introductory part of the new Utopia. His philosophy in some sense amounts to a denial of the possibility of philosophy itself. At least, he maintains that there are no secure and reliable ideas upon which we can rest with a final mental satisfaction. It will be both clearer, however, and more amusing to quote Mr. Wells himself.

He says, "Nothing endures, nothing is precise and certain (except the mind of a pedant).... Being indeed!—there is no being, but a universal becoming of individualities, and Plato turned his back on truth when he turned towards his museum of specific ideals."

Mr. Wells says, again, "There is no abiding thing in what we know. We change from weaker to stronger lights, and each more powerful light pierces our hitherto opaque foundations and reveals fresh and different opacities below." Now, when Mr. Wells says things like this, I speak with all respect when I say that he does not observe an evident mental distinction. It cannot be true that there is nothing abiding in what we know. For if that were so we should not know it all and should not call it knowledge. Our mental state may be very different from that of somebody else some thousands of years back; but it cannot be entirely different, or else we should not be conscious of a difference. Mr. Wells must surely realize the first and simplest of the paradoxes that sit by the springs of truth. He must surely see that the fact of two things being different implies that they are similar. The hare and the tortoise may differ in the quality of swiftness, but they must agree in the quality of motion. The swiftest hare cannot be swifter than an isosceles triangle or the idea of pinkness. When we say the hare moves faster, we say that the tortoise moves. And when we say of a thing that it moves, we say, without need of other words, that there are things that do not move. And even in the act of saying that things change, we say that there is something unchangeable.

But certainly the best example of Mr. Wells's fallacy can be found in the example which he himself chooses. It is quite true that we see a dim light which, compared with a darker thing, is light, but which, compared with a stronger light, is darkness. But the quality of light remains the same thing, or else we should not call it a stronger light or recognize it as such. If the character of light were not fixed in the mind, we should be quite as likely to call a denser shadow a stronger light, or vice versa If the character of light became even for an instant unfixed, if it became even by a hair's-breadth doubtful, if, for example, there crept into our idea of light some vague idea of blueness, then in that flash we have become doubtful whether the new light has more light or less. In brief, the progress may be as varying as a cloud, but the direction must be as rigid as a French road. North and South are relative in the sense that I am North of Bournemouth and South of Spitzbergen. But if there be any doubt of the position of the North Pole, there is in equal degree a doubt of whether I am South of Spitzbergen at all. The absolute idea of light may be practically unattainable. We may not be able to procure pure light. We may not be able to get to the North Pole. But because the North Pole is unattainable, it does not follow that it is indefinable. And it is only because the North Pole is not indefinable that we can make a satisfactory map of Brighton and Worthing.

In other words, Plato turned his face to truth but his back on Mr. H. G. Wells, when he turned to his museum of specified ideals. It is precisely here that Plato shows his sense. It is not true that everything changes; the things that change are all the manifest and material things. There is something that does not change; and that is precisely the abstract quality, the invisible idea. Mr. Wells says truly enough, that a thing which we have seen in one connection as dark we may see in another connection as light. But the thing common to both incidents is the mere idea of light—which we have not seen at all. Mr. Wells might grow taller and taller for unending aeons till his head was higher than the loneliest star. I can imagine his writing a good novel about it. In that case he would see the trees first as tall things and then as short things; he would see the clouds first as high and then as low. But there would remain with him through the ages in that starry loneliness the idea of tallness; he would have in the awful spaces for companion and comfort the definite conception that he was growing taller and not (for instance) growing fatter.

And now it comes to my mind that Mr. H. G. Wells actually has written a very delightful romance about men growing as tall as trees; and that here, again, he seems to me to have been a victim of this vague relativism. "The Food of the Gods" is, like Mr. Bernard Shaw's play, in essence a study of the Superman idea.

And it lies, I think, even through the veil of a half-pantomimic allegory, open to the same intellectual attack. We cannot be expected to have any regard for a great creature if he does not in any manner conform to our standards. For unless he passes our standard of greatness we cannot even call him great. Nietszche summed up all that is interesting in the Superman idea when he said, "Man is a thing which has to be surpassed." But the very word "surpass" implies the existence of a standard common to us and the thing surpassing us. If the Superman is more manly than men are, of course they will ultimately deify him, even if they happen to kill him first. But if he is simply more supermanly, they may be quite indifferent to him as they would be to another seemingly aimless monstrosity. He must submit to our test even in order to overawe us. Mere force or size even is a standard; but that alone will never make men think a man their superior. Giants, as in the wise old fairy-tales, are vermin. Supermen, if not good men, are vermin.

"The Food of the Gods" is the tale of "Jack the Giant-Killer" told from the point of view of the giant. This has not, I think, been done before in literature; but I have little doubt that the psychological substance of it existed in fact. I have little doubt that the giant whom Jack killed did regard himself as the Superman. It is likely enough that he considered Jack a narrow and parochial person who wished to frustrate a great forward movement of the life-force. If (as not unfrequently was the case) he happened to have two heads, he would point out the elementary maxim which declares them to be better than one. He would enlarge on the subtle modernity of such an equipment, enabling a giant to look at a subject from two points of view, or to correct himself with promptitude. But Jack was the champion of the enduring human standards, of the principle of one man one head and one man one conscience, of the single head and the single heart and the single eye. Jack was quite unimpressed by the question of whether the giant was a particularly gigantic giant. All he wished to know was whether he was a good giant—that is, a giant who was any good to us. What were the giant's religious views; what his views on politics and the duties of the citizen? Was he fond of children—or fond of them only in a dark and sinister sense? To use a fine phrase for emotional sanity, was his heart in the right place? Jack had sometimes to cut him up with a sword in order to find out. The old and correct story of Jack the Giant-Killer is simply the whole story of man; if it were understood we should need no Bibles or histories. But the modern world in particular does not seem to understand it at all. The modern world, like Mr. Wells is on the side of the giants; the safest place, and therefore the meanest and the most prosaic. The modern world, when it praises its little Caesars, talks of being strong and brave: but it does not seem to see the eternal paradox involved in the conjunction of these ideas. The strong cannot be brave. Only the weak can be brave; and yet again, in practice, only those who can be brave can be trusted, in time of doubt, to be strong. The only way in which a giant could really keep himself in training against the inevitable Jack would be by continually fighting other giants ten times as big as himself. That is by ceasing to be a giant and becoming a Jack. Thus that sympathy with the small or the defeated as such, with which we Liberals and Nationalists have been often reproached, is not a useless sentimentalism at all, as Mr. Wells and his friends fancy. It is the first law of practical courage. To be in the weakest camp is to be in the strongest school. Nor can I imagine anything that would do humanity more good than the advent of a race of Supermen, for them to fight like dragons. If the Superman is better than we, of course we need not fight him; but in that case, why not call him the Saint? But if he is merely stronger (whether physically, mentally, or morally stronger, I do not care a farthing), then he ought to have to reckon with us at least for all the strength we have. It we are weaker than he, that is no reason why we should be weaker than ourselves. If we are not tall enough to touch the giant's knees, that is no reason why we should become shorter by falling on our own. But that is at bottom the meaning of all modern hero-worship and celebration of the Strong Man, the Caesar the Superman. That he may be something more than man, we must be something less.

Doubtless there is an older and better hero-worship than this. But the old hero was a being who, like Achilles, was more human than humanity itself. Nietzsche's Superman is cold and friendless. Achilles is so foolishly fond of his friend that he slaughters armies in the agony of his bereavement. Mr. Shaw's sad Caesar says in his desolate pride, "He who has never hoped can never despair." The Man-God of old answers from his awful hill, "Was ever sorrow like unto my sorrow?" A great man is not a man so strong that he feels less than other men; he is a man so strong that he feels more. And when Nietszche says, "A new commandment I give to you, 'be hard,'" he is really saying, "A new commandment I give to you, 'be dead.'" Sensibility is the definition of life.

I recur for a last word to Jack the Giant-Killer. I have dwelt on this matter of Mr. Wells and the giants, not because it is specially prominent in his mind; I know that the Superman does not bulk so large in his cosmos as in that of Mr. Bernard Shaw. I have dwelt on it for the opposite reason; because this heresy of immoral hero-worship has taken, I think, a slighter hold of him, and may perhaps still be prevented from perverting one of the best thinkers of the day. In the course of "The New Utopia" Mr. Wells makes more than one admiring allusion to Mr. W. E. Henley. That clever and unhappy man lived in admiration of a vague violence, and was always going back to rude old tales and rude old ballads, to strong and primitive literatures, to find the praise of strength and the justification of tyranny. But he could not find it. It is not there. The primitive literature is shown in the tale of Jack the Giant-Killer. The strong old literature is all in praise of the weak. The rude old tales are as tender to minorities as any modern political idealist. The rude old ballads are as sentimentally concerned for the under-dog as the Aborigines Protection Society. When men were tough and raw, when they lived amid hard knocks and hard laws, when they knew what fighting really was, they had only two kinds of songs. The first was a rejoicing that the weak had conquered the strong, the second a lamentation that the strong had, for once in a way, conquered the weak. For this defiance of the statu quo, this constant effort to alter the existing balance, this premature challenge to the powerful, is the whole nature and inmost secret of the psychological adventure which is called man. It is his strength to disdain strength. The forlorn hope is not only a real hope, it is the only real hope of mankind. In the coarsest ballads of the greenwood men are admired most when they defy, not only the king, but what is more to the point, the hero. The moment Robin Hood becomes a sort of Superman, that moment the chivalrous chronicler shows us Robin thrashed by a poor tinker whom he thought to thrust aside. And the chivalrous chronicler makes Robin Hood receive the thrashing in a glow of admiration. This magnanimity is not a product of modern humanitarianism; it is not a product of anything to do with peace. This magnanimity is merely one of the lost arts of war. The Henleyites call for a sturdy and fighting England, and they go back to the fierce old stories of the sturdy and fighting English. And the thing that they find written across that fierce old literature everywhere, is "the policy of Majuba."

VI. Christmas and the Aesthetes

The world is round, so round that the schools of optimism and pessimism have been arguing from the beginning whether it is the right way up. The difficulty does not arise so much from the mere fact that good and evil are mingled in roughly equal proportions; it arises chiefly from the fact that men always differ about what parts are good and what evil. Hence the difficulty which besets "undenominational religions." They profess to include what is beautiful in all creeds, but they appear to many to have collected all that is dull in them. All the colours mixed together in purity ought to make a perfect white. Mixed together on any human paint-box, they make a thing like mud, and a thing very like many new religions. Such a blend is often something much worse than any one creed taken separately, even the creed of the Thugs. The error arises from the difficulty of detecting what is really the good part and what is really the bad part of any given religion. And this pathos falls rather heavily on those persons who have the misfortune to think of some religion or other, that the parts commonly counted good are bad, and the parts commonly counted bad are good.

It is tragic to admire and honestly admire a human group, but to admire it in a photographic negative. It is difficult to congratulate all their whites on being black and all their blacks on their whiteness. This will often happen to us in connection with human religions. Take two institutions which bear witness to the religious energy of the nineteenth century. Take the Salvation Army and the philosophy of Auguste Comte.

The usual verdict of educated people on the Salvation Army is expressed in some such words as these: "I have no doubt they do a great deal of good, but they do it in a vulgar and profane style; their aims are excellent, but their methods are wrong." To me, unfortunately, the precise reverse of this appears to be the truth. I do not know whether the aims of the Salvation Army are excellent, but I am quite sure their methods are admirable. Their methods are the methods of all intense and hearty religions; they are popular like all religion, military like all religion, public and sensational like all religion. They are not reverent any more than Roman Catholics are reverent, for reverence in the sad and delicate meaning of the term reverence is a thing only possible to infidels. That beautiful twilight you will find in Euripides, in Renan, in Matthew Arnold; but in men who believe you will not find it—you will find only laughter and war. A man cannot pay that kind of reverence to truth solid as marble; they can only be reverent towards a beautiful lie. And the Salvation Army, though their voice has broken out in a mean environment and an ugly shape, are really the old voice of glad and angry faith, hot as the riots of Dionysus, wild as the gargoyles of Catholicism, not to be mistaken for a philosophy. Professor Huxley, in one of his clever phrases, called the Salvation Army "corybantic Christianity." Huxley was the last and noblest of those Stoics who have never understood the Cross. If he had understood Christianity he would have known that there never has been, and never can be, any Christianity that is not corybantic.

And there is this difference between the matter of aims and the matter of methods, that to judge of the aims of a thing like the Salvation Army is very difficult, to judge of their ritual and atmosphere very easy. No one, perhaps, but a sociologist can see whether General Booth's housing scheme is right. But any healthy person can see that banging brass cymbals together must be right. A page of statistics, a plan of model dwellings, anything which is rational, is always difficult for the lay mind. But the thing which is irrational any one can understand. That is why religion came so early into the world and spread so far, while science came so late into the world and has not spread at all. History unanimously attests the fact that it is only mysticism which stands the smallest chance of being understanded of the people. Common sense has to be kept as an esoteric secret in the dark temple of culture. And so while the philanthropy of the Salvationists and its genuineness may be a reasonable matter for the discussion of the doctors, there can be no doubt about the genuineness of their brass bands, for a brass band is purely spiritual, and seeks only to quicken the internal life. The object of philanthropy is to do good; the object of religion is to be good, if only for a moment, amid a crash of brass.

And the same antithesis exists about another modern religion—I mean the religion of Comte, generally known as Positivism, or the worship of humanity. Such men as Mr. Frederic Harrison, that brilliant and chivalrous philosopher, who still, by his mere personality, speaks for the creed, would tell us that he offers us the philosophy of Comte, but not all Comte's fantastic proposals for pontiffs and ceremonials, the new calendar, the new holidays and saints' days. He does not mean that we should dress ourselves up as priests of humanity or let off fireworks because it is Milton's birthday. To the solid English Comtist all this appears, he confesses, to be a little absurd. To me it appears the only sensible part of Comtism. As a philosophy it is unsatisfactory. It is evidently impossible to worship humanity, just as it is impossible to worship the Savile Club; both are excellent institutions to which we may happen to belong. But we perceive clearly that the Savile Club did not make the stars and does not fill the universe. And it is surely unreasonable to attack the doctrine of the Trinity as a piece of bewildering mysticism, and then to ask men to worship a being who is ninety million persons in one God, neither confounding the persons nor dividing the substance.

But if the wisdom of Comte was insufficient, the folly of Comte was wisdom. In an age of dusty modernity, when beauty was thought of as something barbaric and ugliness as something sensible, he alone saw that men must always have the sacredness of mummery. He saw that while the brutes have all the useful things, the things that are truly human are the useless ones. He saw the falsehood of that almost universal notion of to-day, the notion that rites and forms are something artificial, additional, and corrupt. Ritual is really much older than thought; it is much simpler and much wilder than thought. A feeling touching the nature of things does not only make men feel that there are certain proper things to say; it makes them feel that there are certain proper things to do. The more agreeable of these consist of dancing, building temples, and shouting very loud; the less agreeable, of wearing green carnations and burning other philosophers alive. But everywhere the religious dance came before the religious hymn, and man was a ritualist before he could speak. If Comtism had spread the world would have been converted, not by the Comtist philosophy, but by the Comtist calendar. By discouraging what they conceive to be the weakness of their master, the English Positivists have broken the strength of their religion. A man who has faith must be prepared not only to be a martyr, but to be a fool. It is absurd to say that a man is ready to toil and die for his convictions when he is not even ready to wear a wreath round his head for them. I myself, to take a corpus vile, am very certain that I would not read the works of Comte through for any consideration whatever. But I can easily imagine myself with the greatest enthusiasm lighting a bonfire on Darwin Day.

That splendid effort failed, and nothing in the style of it has succeeded. There has been no rationalist festival, no rationalist ecstasy. Men are still in black for the death of God. When Christianity was heavily bombarded in the last century upon no point was it more persistently and brilliantly attacked than upon that of its alleged enmity to human joy. Shelley and Swinburne and all their armies have passed again and again over the ground, but they have not altered it. They have not set up a single new trophy or ensign for the world's merriment to rally to. They have not given a name or a new occasion of gaiety. Mr. Swinburne does not hang up his stocking on the eve of the birthday of Victor Hugo. Mr. William Archer does not sing carols descriptive of the infancy of Ibsen outside people's doors in the snow. In the round of our rational and mournful year one festival remains out of all those ancient gaieties that once covered the whole earth. Christmas remains to remind us of those ages, whether Pagan or Christian, when the many acted poetry instead of the few writing it. In all the winter in our woods there is no tree in glow but the holly.

The strange truth about the matter is told in the very word "holiday." A bank holiday means presumably a day which bankers regard as holy. A half-holiday means, I suppose, a day on which a schoolboy is only partially holy. It is hard to see at first sight why so human a thing as leisure and larkiness should always have a religious origin. Rationally there appears no reason why we should not sing and give each other presents in honour of anything—the birth of Michael Angelo or the opening of Euston Station. But it does not work. As a fact, men only become greedily and gloriously material about something spiritualistic. Take away the Nicene Creed and similar things, and you do some strange wrong to the sellers of sausages. Take away the strange beauty of the saints, and what has remained to us is the far stranger ugliness of Wandsworth. Take away the supernatural, and what remains is the unnatural.

And now I have to touch upon a very sad matter. There are in the modern world an admirable class of persons who really make protest on behalf of that antiqua pulchritudo of which Augustine spoke, who do long for the old feasts and formalities of the childhood of the world. William Morris and his followers showed how much brighter were the dark ages than the age of Manchester. Mr. W. B. Yeats frames his steps in prehistoric dances, but no man knows and joins his voice to forgotten choruses that no one but he can hear. Mr. George Moore collects every fragment of Irish paganism that the forgetfulness of the Catholic Church has left or possibly her wisdom preserved. There are innumerable persons with eye-glasses and green garments who pray for the return of the maypole or the Olympian games. But there is about these people a haunting and alarming something which suggests that it is just possible that they do not keep Christmas. It is painful to regard human nature in such a light, but it seems somehow possible that Mr. George Moore does not wave his spoon and shout when the pudding is set alight. It is even possible that Mr. W. B. Yeats never pulls crackers. If so, where is the sense of all their dreams of festive traditions? Here is a solid and ancient festive tradition still plying a roaring trade in the streets, and they think it vulgar. if this is so, let them be very certain of this, that they are the kind of people who in the time of the maypole would have thought the maypole vulgar; who in the time of the Canterbury pilgrimage would have thought the Canterbury pilgrimage vulgar; who in the time of the Olympian games would have thought the Olympian games vulgar. Nor can there be any reasonable doubt that they were vulgar. Let no man deceive himself; if by vulgarity we mean coarseness of speech, rowdiness of behaviour, gossip, horseplay, and some heavy drinking, vulgarity there always was wherever there was joy, wherever there was faith in the gods. Wherever you have belief you will have hilarity, wherever you have hilarity you will have some dangers. And as creed and mythology produce this gross and vigorous life, so in its turn this gross and vigorous life will always produce creed and mythology. If we ever get the English back on to the English land they will become again a religious people, if all goes well, a superstitious people. The absence from modern life of both the higher and lower forms of faith is largely due to a divorce from nature and the trees and clouds. If we have no more turnip ghosts it is chiefly from the lack of turnips.

VII. Omar and the Sacred Vine

A new morality has burst upon us with some violence in connection with the problem of strong drink; and enthusiasts in the matter range from the man who is violently thrown out at 12.30, to the lady who smashes American bars with an axe. In these discussions it is almost always felt that one very wise and moderate position is to say that wine or such stuff should only be drunk as a medicine. With this I should venture to disagree with a peculiar ferocity. The one genuinely dangerous and immoral way of drinking wine is to drink it as a medicine. And for this reason, If a man drinks wine in order to obtain pleasure, he is trying to obtain something exceptional, something he does not expect every hour of the day, something which, unless he is a little insane, he will not try to get every hour of the day. But if a man drinks wine in order to obtain health, he is trying to get something natural; something, that is, that he ought not to be without; something that he may find it difficult to reconcile himself to being without. The man may not be seduced who has seen the ecstasy of being ecstatic; it is more dazzling to catch a glimpse of the ecstasy of being ordinary. If there were a magic ointment, and we took it to a strong man, and said, "This will enable you to jump off the Monument," doubtless he would jump off the Monument, but he would not jump off the Monument all day long to the delight of the City. But if we took it to a blind man, saying, "This will enable you to see," he would be under a heavier temptation. It would be hard for him not to rub it on his eyes whenever he heard the hoof of a noble horse or the birds singing at daybreak. It is easy to deny one's self festivity; it is difficult to deny one's self normality. Hence comes the fact which every doctor knows, that it is often perilous to give alcohol to the sick even when they need it. I need hardly say that I do not mean that I think the giving of alcohol to the sick for stimulus is necessarily unjustifiable. But I do mean that giving it to the healthy for fun is the proper use of it, and a great deal more consistent with health.

The sound rule in the matter would appear to be like many other sound rules—a paradox. Drink because you are happy, but never because you are miserable. Never drink when you are wretched without it, or you will be like the grey-faced gin-drinker in the slum; but drink when you would be happy without it, and you will be like the laughing peasant of Italy. Never drink because you need it, for this is rational drinking, and the way to death and hell. But drink because you do not need it, for this is irrational drinking, and the ancient health of the world.

For more than thirty years the shadow and glory of a great Eastern figure has lain upon our English literature. Fitzgerald's translation of Omar Khayyam concentrated into an immortal poignancy all the dark and drifting hedonism of our time. Of the literary splendour of that work it would be merely banal to speak; in few other of the books of men has there been anything so combining the gay pugnacity of an epigram with the vague sadness of a song. But of its philosophical, ethical, and religious influence which has been almost as great as its brilliancy, I should like to say a word, and that word, I confess, one of uncompromising hostility. There are a great many things which might be said against the spirit of the Rubaiyat, and against its prodigious influence. But one matter of indictment towers ominously above the rest—a genuine disgrace to it, a genuine calamity to us. This is the terrible blow that this great poem has struck against sociability and the joy of life. Some one called Omar "the sad, glad old Persian." Sad he is; glad he is not, in any sense of the word whatever. He has been a worse foe to gladness than the Puritans.

A pensive and graceful Oriental lies under the rose-tree with his wine-pot and his scroll of poems. It may seem strange that any one's thoughts should, at the moment of regarding him, fly back to the dark bedside where the doctor doles out brandy. It may seem stranger still that they should go back to the grey wastrel shaking with gin in Houndsditch. But a great philosophical unity links the three in an evil bond. Omar Khayyam's wine-bibbing is bad, not because it is wine-bibbing. It is bad, and very bad, because it is medical wine-bibbing. It is the drinking of a man who drinks because he is not happy. His is the wine that shuts out the universe, not the wine that reveals it. It is not poetical drinking, which is joyous and instinctive; it is rational drinking, which is as prosaic as an investment, as unsavoury as a dose of camomile. Whole heavens above it, from the point of view of sentiment, though not of style, rises the splendour of some old English drinking-song—

> "Then pass the bowl, my comrades all,
> And let the zider vlow."

For this song was caught up by happy men to express the worth of truly worthy things, of brotherhood and garrulity, and the brief and kindly leisure of the poor. Of course, the great part of the more stolid reproaches directed against the Omarite morality are as false and babyish as such reproaches usually are. One critic, whose work I have read, had the incredible foolishness to call Omar an atheist and a materialist. It is almost impossible for an Oriental to be either; the East understands metaphysics too well for that. Of course, the real objection which a philosophical Christian would bring against the religion of Omar, is not that he gives no place to God, it is that he gives too much place to God. His is that terrible theism which can imagine nothing else but deity, and which denies altogether the outlines of human personality and human will.

> "The ball no question makes of Ayes or Noes,
> But Here or There as strikes the Player goes;
> And He that tossed you down into the field,
> He knows about it all—he knows—he knows."

A Christian thinker such as Augustine or Dante would object to this because it ignores free-will, which is the valour and dignity of the soul. The quarrel of the highest Christianity with this scepticism is not in the least that the scepticism denies the existence of God; it is that it denies the existence of man.

In this cult of the pessimistic pleasure-seeker the Rubaiyat stands first in our time; but it does not stand alone. Many of the most brilliant intellects of our time have urged us to the same self-conscious snatching at a rare delight. Walter Pater said that we were all under sentence of death, and the only course was to enjoy exquisite moments simply for those moments' sake. The same lesson was taught by the very powerful and very desolate philosophy of Oscar Wilde. It is the carpe diem religion; but the carpe diem religion is not the religion of happy people, but of very unhappy people. Great joy does, not gather the rosebuds while it may; its eyes are fixed on the immortal rose which Dante saw. Great joy has in it the sense of immortality; the very splendour of youth is the sense that it has all space to stretch its legs in. In all great comic literature, in "Tristram Shandy" or "Pickwick", there is this sense of space and incorruptibility; we feel the characters are deathless people in an endless tale.

It is true enough, of course, that a pungent happiness comes chiefly in certain passing moments; but it is not true that we should think of them as passing, or enjoy them simply "for those moments' sake." To do this is to rationalize the happiness, and therefore to destroy it. Happiness is a mystery like religion, and should never be rationalized. Suppose a man experiences a really splendid moment of pleasure. I do not mean something connected with a bit of enamel, I mean something with a violent happiness in it—an almost painful happiness. A man may have, for instance, a moment of ecstasy in first love, or a moment of victory in battle. The lover enjoys the moment, but precisely not for the moment's sake. He enjoys it for the woman's sake, or his own sake. The warrior enjoys the moment, but not for the sake of the moment; he enjoys it for the sake of the flag. The cause which the flag stands for may be foolish and fleeting; the love may be calf-love, and last a week. But the patriot thinks of the flag as eternal; the lover thinks of his love as something that cannot end. These moments are filled with eternity; these moments are joyful because they do not seem momentary. Once look at them as moments after Pater's manner, and they become as cold as Pater and his style. Man cannot love mortal things. He can only love immortal things for an instant.

Pater's mistake is revealed in his most famous phrase. He asks us to burn with a hard, gem-like flame. Flames are never hard and never gem-like—they cannot be handled or arranged. So human emotions are never hard and never gem-like; they are always dangerous, like flames, to touch or even to examine. There is only one way in which our passions can become hard and gem-like, and that is by becoming as cold as gems. No blow then has ever been struck at the natural loves and laughter of men so sterilizing as this carpe diem of the aesthetes. For any kind of pleasure a totally different spirit is required; a certain shyness, a certain indeterminate hope, a certain boyish expectation. Purity and simplicity are essential to passions—yes even to evil passions. Even vice demands a sort of virginity.

Omar's (or Fitzgerald's) effect upon the other world we may let go, his hand upon this world has been heavy and paralyzing. The Puritans, as I have said, are far jollier than he. The new ascetics who follow Thoreau or Tolstoy are much livelier company; for, though the surrender of strong drink and such luxuries may strike us as an idle negation, it may leave a man with innumerable natural pleasures, and, above all, with man's natural power of happiness. Thoreau could enjoy the sunrise without a cup of coffee. If Tolstoy cannot admire marriage, at least he is healthy enough to admire mud. Nature can be enjoyed without even the most natural luxuries. A good bush needs no wine. But neither nature nor wine nor anything else can be enjoyed if we have the wrong attitude towards happiness, and Omar (or Fitzgerald) did have the wrong attitude towards happiness. He and those he has influenced do not see that if we are to be truly gay, we must believe that there is some eternal gaiety in the nature of things. We cannot enjoy thoroughly even a pas-de-quatre at a subscription dance unless we believe that the stars are dancing to the same tune. No one can be really hilarious but the serious man. "Wine," says the Scripture, "maketh glad the heart of man," but only of the man who has a heart. The thing called high spirits is possible only to the spiritual. Ultimately a man cannot rejoice in anything except the nature of things. Ultimately a man can enjoy nothing except religion. Once in the world's history men did believe that the stars were dancing to the tune of their temples, and they danced as men have never danced since. With this old pagan eudaemonism the sage of the Rubaiyat has quite as little to do as he has with any Christian variety. He is no more a Bacchanal than he is a saint. Dionysus and his church was grounded on a serious joie-de-vivre like that of Walt Whitman. Dionysus made wine, not a medicine, but a sacrament. Jesus Christ also made wine, not a medicine, but a sacrament. But Omar makes it, not a sacrament, but a medicine. He feasts because life is not joyful; he revels because he is not glad. "Drink," he says, "for you know not whence you come nor why. Drink, for you know not when you go nor where. Drink, because the stars are cruel and the world as idle as a humming-top. Drink, because there is nothing worth trusting, nothing worth fighting for. Drink, because all things are lapsed in a base equality and an evil peace." So he stands offering us the cup in his hand. And at the high altar of Christianity stands another figure, in whose hand also is the cup of the vine. "Drink" he says "for the whole world is as red as this wine, with the crimson of the love and wrath of God. Drink, for the trumpets are blowing for battle and this is the stirrup-cup. Drink, for this my blood of the new testament that is shed for you. Drink, for I know of whence you come and why. Drink, for I know of when you go and where."

VIII. The Mildness of the Yellow Press

There is a great deal of protest made from one quarter or another nowadays against the influence of that new journalism which is associated with the names of Sir Alfred Harmsworth and Mr. Pearson. But almost everybody who attacks it attacks on the ground that it is very sensational, very violent and vulgar and startling. I am speaking in no affected contrariety, but in the simplicity of a genuine personal impression, when I say that this journalism offends as being not sensational or violent enough. The real vice is not that it is startling, but that it is quite insupportably tame. The whole object is to keep carefully along a certain level of the expected and the commonplace; it may be low, but it must take care also to be flat. Never by any chance in it is there any of that real plebeian pungency which can be heard from the ordinary cabman in the ordinary street. We have heard of a certain standard of decorum which demands that things should be funny without being vulgar, but the standard of this decorum demands that if things are vulgar they shall be vulgar without being funny. This journalism does not merely fail to exaggerate life—it positively underrates it; and it has to do so because it is intended for the faint and languid recreation of men whom the fierceness of modern life has fatigued. This press is not the yellow press at all; it is the drab press. Sir Alfred Harmsworth must not address to the tired clerk any observation more witty than the tired clerk might be able to address to Sir Alfred Harmsworth. It must not expose anybody (anybody who is powerful, that is), it must not offend anybody, it must not even please anybody, too much. A general vague idea that in spite of all this, our yellow press is sensational, arises from such external accidents as large type or lurid headlines. It is quite true that these editors print everything they possibly can in large capital letters. But they do this, not because it is startling, but because it is soothing. To people wholly weary or partly drunk in a dimly lighted train, it is a simplification and a comfort to have things presented in this vast and obvious manner. The editors use this gigantic alphabet in dealing with their readers, for exactly the same reason that parents and governesses use a similar gigantic alphabet in teaching children to spell. The nursery authorities do not use an A as big as a horseshoe in order to make the child jump; on the contrary, they use it to put the child at his ease, to make things smoother and more evident. Of the same character is the dim and quiet dame school which Sir Alfred Harmsworth and Mr. Pearson keep. All their sentiments are spelling-book sentiments—that is to say, they are sentiments with which the pupil is already respectfully familiar. All their wildest posters are leaves torn from a copy-book.

Of real sensational journalism, as it exists in France, in Ireland, and in America, we have no trace in this country. When a journalist in Ireland wishes to create a thrill, he creates a thrill worth talking about. He denounces a leading Irish member for corruption, or he charges the whole police system with a wicked and definite conspiracy. When a French journalist desires a frisson there is a frisson; he discovers, let us say, that the President of the Republic has murdered three wives. Our yellow journalists invent quite as unscrupulously as this; their moral condition is, as regards careful veracity, about the same. But it is their mental calibre which happens to be such that they can only invent calm and even reassuring things. The fictitious version of the massacre of the envoys of Pekin was mendacious, but it was not interesting, except to those who had private reasons for terror or sorrow. It was not connected with any bold and suggestive view of the Chinese situation. It revealed only a vague idea that nothing could be impressive except a great deal of blood. Real sensationalism, of which I happen to be very fond, may be either moral or immoral. But even when it is most immoral, it requires moral courage. For it is one of the most dangerous things on earth genuinely to surprise anybody. If you make any sentient creature jump, you render it by no means improbable that it will jump on you. But the leaders of this movement have no moral courage or immoral courage; their whole method consists in saying, with large and elaborate emphasis, the things which everybody else says casually, and without remembering what they have said. When they brace themselves up to attack anything, they never reach the point of attacking anything which is large and real, and would resound with the shock. They do not attack the army as men do in France, or the judges as men do in Ireland, or the democracy itself as men did in England a hundred years ago. They attack something like the War Office—something, that is, which everybody attacks and nobody bothers to defend, something which is an old joke in fourth-rate comic papers. just as a man shows he has a weak voice by straining it to shout, so they show the hopelessly unsensational nature of their minds when they really try to be sensational. With the whole world full of big and dubious institutions, with the whole wickedness of civilization staring them in the face, their idea of being bold and bright is to attack the War Office. They might as well start a campaign against the weather, or form a secret society in order to make jokes about mothers-in-law. Nor is it only from the point of view of particular amateurs of the sensational such as myself, that it is permissible to say, in the words of Cowper's Alexander Selkirk, that "their tameness is shocking to me." The whole modern world is pining for a genuinely sensational journalism. This has been discovered by that very able and honest journalist, Mr. Blatchford, who started his campaign against Christianity, warned on all sides, I believe, that it would ruin his paper, but who continued from an honourable sense of intellectual responsibility. He discovered, however, that while he had undoubtedly shocked his readers, he had also greatly advanced his newspaper. It was bought—first, by all the people who agreed with him and wanted to read it; and secondly, by all the people who disagreed with him, and wanted to write him letters. Those letters were voluminous (I helped, I am glad to say, to swell their volume), and they were generally inserted with a generous fulness. Thus was accidentally discovered (like the steam-engine) the great journalistic maxim—that if an editor can only make people angry enough, they will write half his newspaper for him for nothing.

Some hold that such papers as these are scarcely the proper objects of so serious a consideration; but that can scarcely be maintained from a political or ethical point of view. In this problem of the mildness and tameness of the Harmsworth mind there is mirrored the outlines of a much larger problem which is akin to it.

The Harmsworthian journalist begins with a worship of success and violence, and ends in sheer timidity and mediocrity. But he is not alone in this, nor does he come by this fate merely because he happens personally to be stupid. Every man, however brave, who begins by worshipping violence, must end in mere timidity. Every man, however wise, who begins by worshipping success, must end in mere mediocrity. This strange and paradoxical fate is involved, not in the individual, but in the philosophy, in the point of view. It is not the folly of the man which brings about this necessary fall; it is his wisdom. The worship of success is the only one out of all possible worships of which this is true, that its followers are foredoomed to become slaves and cowards. A man may be a hero for the sake of Mrs. Gallup's ciphers or for the sake of human sacrifice, but not for the sake of success. For obviously a man may choose to fail because he loves Mrs. Gallup or human sacrifice; but he cannot choose to fail because he loves success. When the test of triumph is men's test of everything, they never endure long enough to triumph at all. As long as matters are really hopeful, hope is a mere flattery or platitude; it is only when everything is hopeless that hope begins to be a strength at all. Like all the Christian virtues, it is as unreasonable as it is indispensable.

It was through this fatal paradox in the nature of things that all these modern adventurers come at last to a sort of tedium and acquiescence. They desired strength; and to them to desire strength was to admire strength; to admire strength was simply to admire the statu quo. They thought that he who wished to be strong ought to respect the strong. They did not realize the obvious verity that he who wishes to be strong must despise the strong. They sought to be everything, to have the whole force of the cosmos behind them, to have an energy that would drive the stars. But they did not realize the two great facts—first, that in the attempt to be everything the first and most difficult step is to be something; second, that the moment a man is something, he is essentially defying everything. The lower animals, say the men of science, fought their way up with a blind selfishness. If this be so, the only real moral of it is that our unselfishness, if it is to triumph, must be equally blind. The mammoth did not put his head on one side and wonder whether mammoths were a little out of date. Mammoths were at least as much up to date as that individual mammoth could make them. The great elk did not say, "Cloven hoofs are very much worn now." He polished his own weapons for his own use. But in the reasoning animal there has arisen a more horrible danger, that he may fail through perceiving his own failure. When modern sociologists talk of the necessity of accommodating one's self to the trend of the time, they forget that the trend of the time at its best consists entirely of people who will not accommodate themselves to anything. At its worst it consists of many millions of frightened creatures all accommodating themselves to a trend that is not there. And that is becoming more and more the situation of modern England. Every man speaks of public opinion, and means by public opinion, public opinion minus his opinion. Every man makes his contribution negative under the erroneous impression that the next man's contribution is positive. Every man surrenders his fancy to a general tone which is itself a surrender. And over all the heartless and fatuous unity spreads this new and wearisome and platitudinous press, incapable of invention, incapable of audacity, capable only of a servility all the more contemptible because it is not even a servility to the strong. But all who begin with force and conquest will end in this.

The chief characteristic of the "New journalism" is simply that it is bad journalism. It is beyond all comparison the most shapeless, careless, and colourless work done in our day.

I read yesterday a sentence which should be written in letters of gold and adamant; it is the very motto of the new philosophy of Empire. I found it (as the reader has already eagerly guessed) in Pearson's Magazine, while I was communing (soul to soul) with Mr. C. Arthur Pearson, whose first and suppressed name I am afraid is Chilperic. It occurred in an article on the American Presidential Election. This is the sentence, and every one should read it carefully, and roll it on the tongue, till all the honey be tasted.

"A little sound common sense often goes further with an audience of American working-men than much high-flown argument. A speaker who, as he brought forward his points, hammered nails into a board, won hundreds of votes for his side at the last Presidential Election."

I do not wish to soil this perfect thing with comment; the words of Mercury are harsh after the songs of Apollo. But just think for a moment of the mind, the strange inscrutable mind, of the man who wrote that, of the editor who approved it, of the people who are probably impressed by it, of the incredible American working-man, of whom, for all I know, it may be true. Think what their notion of "common sense" must be! It is delightful to realize that you and I are now able to win thousands of votes should we ever be engaged in a Presidential Election, by doing something of this kind. For I suppose the nails and the board are not essential to the exhibition of "common sense;" there may be variations. We may read—

"A little common sense impresses American working-men more than high-flown argument. A speaker who, as he made his points, pulled buttons off his waistcoat, won thousands of votes for his side." Or, "Sound common sense tells better in America than high-flown argument. Thus Senator Budge, who threw his false teeth in the air every time he made an epigram, won the solid approval of American working-men." Or again, "The sound common sense of a gentleman from Earlswood, who stuck straws in his hair during the progress of his speech, assured the victory of Mr. Roosevelt."

There are many other elements in this article on which I should love to linger. But the matter which I wish to point out is that in that sentence is perfectly revealed the whole truth of what our Chamberlainites, hustlers, bustlers, Empire-builders, and strong, silent men, really mean by "commonsense." They mean knocking, with deafening noise and dramatic effect, meaningless bits of iron into a useless bit of wood. A man goes on to an American platform and behaves like a mountebank fool with a board and a hammer; well, I do not blame him; I might even admire him. He may be a dashing and quite decent strategist. He may be a fine romantic actor, like Burke flinging the dagger on the floor. He may even (for all I know) be a sublime mystic, profoundly impressed with the ancient meaning of the divine trade of the Carpenter, and offering to the people a parable in the form of a ceremony. All I wish to indicate is the abyss of mental confusion in which such wild ritualism can be called "sound common sense." And it is in that abyss of mental confusion, and in that alone, that the new Imperialism lives and moves and has its being. The whole glory and greatness of Mr. Chamberlain consists in this: that if a man hits the right nail on the head nobody cares where he hits it to or what it does. They care about the noise of the hammer, not about the silent drip of the nail. Before and throughout the African war, Mr. Chamberlain was always knocking in nails, with ringing decisiveness. But when we ask, "But what have these nails held together? Where is your carpentry? Where are your contented Outlanders? Where is your free South Africa? Where is your British prestige? What have your nails done?" then what answer is there? We must go back (with an affectionate sigh) to our Pearson for the answer to the question of what the nails have done: "The speaker who hammered nails into a board won thousands of votes."

Now the whole of this passage is admirably characteristic of the new journalism which Mr. Pearson represents, the new journalism which has just purchased the Standard. To take one instance out of hundreds, the incomparable man with the board and nails is described in the Pearson's article as calling out (as he smote the symbolic nail), "Lie number one. Nailed to the Mast! Nailed to the Mast!" In the whole office there was apparently no compositor or office-boy to point out that we speak of lies being nailed to the counter, and not to the mast. Nobody in the office knew that Pearson's Magazine was falling into a stale Irish bull, which must be as old as St. Patrick. This is the real and essential tragedy of the sale of the Standard. It is not merely that journalism is victorious over literature. It is that bad journalism is victorious over good journalism.

It is not that one article which we consider costly and beautiful is being ousted by another kind of article which we consider common or unclean. It is that of the same article a worse quality is preferred to a better. If you like popular journalism (as I do), you will know that Pearson's Magazine is poor and weak popular journalism. You will know it as certainly as you know bad butter. You will know as certainly that it is poor popular journalism as you know that the Strand, in the great days of Sherlock Holmes, was good popular journalism. Mr. Pearson has been a monument of this enormous banality. About everything he says and does there is something infinitely weak-minded. He clamours for home trades and employs foreign ones to print his paper. When this glaring fact is pointed out, he does not say that the thing was an oversight, like a sane man. He cuts it off with scissors, like a child of three. His very cunning is infantile. And like a child of three, he does not cut it quite off. In all human records I doubt if there is such an example of a profound simplicity in deception. This is the sort of intelligence which now sits in the seat of the sane and honourable old Tory journalism. If it were really the triumph of the tropical exuberance of the Yankee press, it would be vulgar, but still tropical. But it is not. We are delivered over to the bramble, and from the meanest of the shrubs comes the fire upon the cedars of Lebanon.

The only question now is how much longer the fiction will endure that journalists of this order represent public opinion. It may be doubted whether any honest and serious Tariff Reformer would for a moment maintain that there was any majority for Tariff Reform in the country comparable to the ludicrous preponderance which money has given it among the great dailies. The only inference is that for purposes of real public opinion the press is now a mere plutocratic oligarchy. Doubtless the public buys the wares of these men, for one reason or another. But there is no more reason to suppose that the public admires their politics than that the public admires the delicate philosophy of Mr. Crosse or the darker and sterner creed of Mr. Blackwell. If these men are merely tradesmen, there is nothing to say except that there are plenty like them in the Battersea Park Road, and many much better. But if they make any sort of attempt to be politicians, we can only point out to them that they are not as yet even good journalists.

IX. The Moods of Mr. George Moore

Mr. George Moore began his literary career by writing his personal confessions; nor is there any harm in this if he had not continued them for the remainder of his life. He is a man of genuinely forcible mind and of great command over a kind of rhetorical and fugitive conviction which excites and pleases. He is in a perpetual state of temporary honesty. He has admired all the most admirable modern eccentrics until they could stand it no longer. Everything he writes, it is to be fully admitted, has a genuine mental power. His account of his reason for leaving the Roman Catholic Church is possibly the most admirable tribute to that communion which has been written of late years. For the fact of the matter is, that the weakness which has rendered barren the many brilliancies of Mr. Moore is actually that weakness which the Roman Catholic Church is at its best in combating. Mr. Moore hates Catholicism because it breaks up the house of looking-glasses in which he lives. Mr. Moore does not dislike so much being asked to believe in the spiritual existence of miracles or sacraments, but he does fundamentally dislike being asked to believe in the actual existence of other people. Like his master Pater and all the aesthetes, his real quarrel with life is that it is not a dream that can be moulded by the dreamer. It is not the dogma of the reality of the other world that troubles him, but the dogma of the reality of this world.

The truth is that the tradition of Christianity (which is still the only coherent ethic of Europe) rests on two or three paradoxes or mysteries which can easily be impugned in argument and as easily justified in life. One of them, for instance, is the paradox of hope or faith—that the more hopeless is the situation the more hopeful must be the man. Stevenson understood this, and consequently Mr. Moore cannot understand Stevenson. Another is the paradox of charity or chivalry that the weaker a thing is the more it should be respected, that the more indefensible a thing is the more it should appeal to us for a certain kind of defence. Thackeray understood this, and therefore Mr. Moore does not understand Thackeray. Now, one of these very practical and working mysteries in the Christian tradition, and one which the Roman Catholic Church, as I say, has done her best work in singling out, is the conception of the sinfulness of pride. Pride is a weakness in the character; it dries up laughter, it dries up wonder, it dries up chivalry and energy. The Christian tradition understands this; therefore Mr. Moore does not understand the Christian tradition.

For the truth is much stranger even than it appears in the formal doctrine of the sin of pride. It is not only true that humility is a much wiser and more vigorous thing than pride. It is also true that vanity is a much wiser and more vigorous thing than pride. Vanity is social—it is almost a kind of comradeship; pride is solitary and uncivilized. Vanity is active; it desires the applause of infinite multitudes; pride is passive, desiring only the applause of one person, which it already has. Vanity is humorous, and can enjoy the joke even of itself; pride is dull, and cannot even smile. And the whole of this difference is the difference between Stevenson and Mr. George Moore, who, as he informs us, has "brushed Stevenson aside." I do not know where he has been brushed to, but wherever it is I fancy he is having a good time, because he had the wisdom to be vain, and not proud. Stevenson had a windy vanity; Mr. Moore has a dusty egoism. Hence Stevenson could amuse himself as well as us with his vanity; while the richest effects of Mr. Moore's absurdity are hidden from his eyes.

If we compare this solemn folly with the happy folly with which Stevenson belauds his own books and berates his own critics, we shall not find it difficult to guess why it is that Stevenson at least found a final philosophy of some sort to live by, while Mr. Moore is always walking the world looking for a new one. Stevenson had found that the secret of life lies in laughter and humility. Self is the gorgon. Vanity sees it in the mirror of other men and lives. Pride studies it for itself and is turned to stone.

It is necessary to dwell on this defect in Mr. Moore, because it is really the weakness of work which is not without its strength. Mr. Moore's egoism is not merely a moral weakness, it is a very constant and influential aesthetic weakness as well. We should really be much more interested in Mr. Moore if he were not quite so interested in himself. We feel as if we were being shown through a gallery of really fine pictures, into each of which, by some useless and discordant convention, the artist had represented the same figure in the same attitude. "The Grand Canal with a distant view of Mr. Moore," "Effect of Mr. Moore through a Scotch Mist," "Mr. Moore by Firelight," "Ruins of Mr. Moore by Moonlight," and so on, seems to be the endless series. He would no doubt reply that in such a book as this he intended to reveal himself. But the answer is that in such a book as this he does not succeed. One of the thousand objections to the sin of pride lies precisely in this, that self-consciousness of necessity destroys self-revelation. A man who thinks a great deal about himself will try to be many-sided, attempt a theatrical excellence at all points, will try to be an encyclopaedia of culture, and his own real personality will be lost in that false universalism. Thinking about himself will lead to trying to be the universe; trying to be the universe will lead to ceasing to be anything. If, on the other hand, a man is sensible enough to think only about the universe; he will think about it in his own individual way. He will keep virgin the secret of God; he will see the grass as no other man can see it, and look at a sun that no man has ever known. This fact is very practically brought out in Mr. Moore's "Confessions." In reading them we do not feel the presence of a clean-cut personality like that of Thackeray and Matthew Arnold. We only read a number of quite clever and largely conflicting opinions which might be uttered by any clever person, but which we are called upon to admire specifically, because they are uttered by Mr. Moore. He is the only thread that connects Catholicism and Protestantism, realism and mysticism—he or rather his name. He is profoundly absorbed even in views he no longer holds, and he expects us to be. And he intrudes the capital "I" even where it need not be intruded—even where it weakens the force of a plain statement. Where another man would say, "It is a fine day," Mr. Moore says, "Seen through my temperament, the day appeared fine." Where another man would say "Milton has obviously a fine style," Mr. Moore would say, "As a stylist Milton had always impressed me." The Nemesis of this self-centred spirit is that of being totally ineffectual. Mr. Moore has started many interesting crusades, but he has abandoned them before his disciples could begin. Even when he is on the side of the truth he is as fickle as the children of falsehood. Even when he has found reality he cannot find rest. One Irish quality he has which no Irishman was ever without—pugnacity; and that is certainly a great virtue, especially in the present age. But he has not the tenacity of conviction which goes with the fighting spirit in a man like Bernard Shaw. His weakness of introspection and selfishness in all their glory cannot prevent him fighting; but they will always prevent him winning.

X. On Sandals and Simplicity

The great misfortune of the modern English is not at all that they are more boastful than other people (they are not); it is that they are boastful about those particular things which nobody can boast of without losing them. A Frenchman can be proud of being bold and logical, and still remain bold and logical. A German can be proud of being reflective and orderly, and still remain reflective and orderly. But an Englishman cannot be proud of being simple and direct, and still remain simple and direct. In the matter of these strange virtues, to know them is to kill them. A man may be conscious of being heroic or conscious of being divine, but he cannot (in spite of all the Anglo-Saxon poets) be conscious of being unconscious.

Now, I do not think that it can be honestly denied that some portion of this impossibility attaches to a class very different in their own opinion, at least, to the school of Anglo-Saxonism. I mean that school of the simple life, commonly associated with Tolstoy. If a perpetual talk about one's own robustness leads to being less robust, it is even more true that a perpetual talking about one's own simplicity leads to being less simple. One great complaint, I think, must stand against the modern upholders of the simple life—the simple life in all its varied forms, from vegetarianism to the honourable consistency of the Doukhobors. This complaint against them stands, that they would make us simple in the unimportant things, but complex in the important things. They would make us simple in the things that do not matter—that is, in diet, in costume, in etiquette, in economic system. But they would make us complex in the things that do matter—in philosophy, in loyalty, in spiritual acceptance, and spiritual rejection. It does not so very much matter whether a man eats a grilled tomato or a plain tomato; it does very much matter whether he eats a plain tomato with a grilled mind. The only kind of simplicity worth preserving is the simplicity of the heart, the simplicity which accepts and enjoys. There may be a reasonable doubt as to what system preserves this; there can surely be no doubt that a system of simplicity destroys it. There is more simplicity in the man who eats caviar on impulse than in the man who eats grape-nuts on principle. The chief error of these people is to be found in the very phrase to which they are most attached —"plain living and high thinking." These people do not stand in need of, will not be improved by, plain living and high thinking. They stand in need of the contrary. They would be improved by high living and plain thinking. A little high living (I say, having a full sense of responsibility, a little high living) would teach them the force and meaning of the human festivities, of the banquet that has gone on from the beginning of the world. It would teach them the historic fact that the artificial is, if anything, older than the natural. It would teach them that the loving-cup is as old as any hunger. It would teach them that ritualism is older than any religion. And a little plain thinking would teach them how harsh and fanciful are the mass of their own ethics, how very civilized and very complicated must be the brain of the Tolstoyan who really believes it to be evil to love one's country and wicked to strike a blow.

A man approaches, wearing sandals and simple raiment, a raw tomato held firmly in his right hand, and says, "The affections of family and country alike are hindrances to the fuller development of human love;" but the plain thinker will only answer him, with a wonder not untinged with admiration, "What a great deal of trouble you must have taken in order to feel like that." High living will reject the tomato. Plain thinking will equally decisively reject the idea of the invariable sinfulness of war. High living will convince us that nothing is more materialistic than to despise a pleasure as purely material. And plain thinking will convince us that nothing is more materialistic than to reserve our horror chiefly for material wounds.

The only simplicity that matters is the simplicity of the heart. If that be gone, it can be brought back by no turnips or cellular clothing; but only by tears and terror and the fires that are not quenched. If that remain, it matters very little if a few Early Victorian armchairs remain along with it. Let us put a complex entree into a simple old gentleman; let us not put a simple entree into a complex old gentleman. So long as human society will leave my spiritual inside alone, I will allow it, with a comparative submission, to work its wild will with my physical interior. I will submit to cigars. I will meekly embrace a bottle of Burgundy. I will humble myself to a hansom cab. If only by this means I may preserve to myself the virginity of the spirit, which enjoys with astonishment and fear. I do not say that these are the only methods of preserving it. I incline to the belief that there are others. But I will have nothing to do with simplicity which lacks the fear, the astonishment, and the joy alike. I will have nothing to do with the devilish vision of a child who is too simple to like toys.

The child is, indeed, in these, and many other matters, the best guide. And in nothing is the child so righteously childlike, in nothing does he exhibit more accurately the sounder order of simplicity, than in the fact that he sees everything with a simple pleasure, even the complex things. The false type of naturalness harps always on the distinction between the natural and the artificial. The higher kind of naturalness ignores that distinction. To the child the tree and the lamp-post are as natural and as artificial as each other; or rather, neither of them are natural but both supernatural. For both are splendid and unexplained. The flower with which God crowns the one, and the flame with which Sam the lamplighter crowns the other, are equally of the gold of fairy-tales. In the middle of the wildest fields the most rustic child is, ten to one, playing at steam-engines. And the only spiritual or philosophical objection to steam-engines is not that men pay for them or work at them, or make them very ugly, or even that men are killed by them; but merely that men do not play at them. The evil is that the childish poetry of clockwork does not remain. The wrong is not that engines are too much admired, but that they are not admired enough. The sin is not that engines are mechanical, but that men are mechanical.

In this matter, then, as in all the other matters treated in this book, our main conclusion is that it is a fundamental point of view, a philosophy or religion which is needed, and not any change in habit or social routine. The things we need most for immediate practical purposes are all abstractions. We need a right view of the human lot, a right view of the human society; and if we were living eagerly and angrily in the enthusiasm of those things, we should, ipso facto, be living simply in the genuine and spiritual sense. Desire and danger make every one simple. And to those who talk to us with interfering eloquence about Jaeger and the pores of the skin, and about Plasmon and the coats of the stomach, at them shall only be hurled the words that are hurled at fops and gluttons, "Take no thought what ye shall eat or what ye shall drink, or wherewithal ye shall be clothed. For after all these things do the Gentiles seek. But seek first the kingdom of God and His righteousness, and all these things shall be added unto you." Those amazing words are not only extraordinarily good, practical politics; they are also superlatively good hygiene. The one supreme way of making all those processes go right, the processes of health, and strength, and grace, and beauty, the one and only way of making certain of their accuracy, is to think about something else. If a man is bent on climbing into the seventh heaven, he may be quite easy about the pores of his skin. If he harnesses his waggon to a star, the process will have a most satisfactory effect upon the coats of his stomach. For the thing called "taking thought," the thing for which the best modern word is "rationalizing," is in its nature, inapplicable to all plain and urgent things. Men take thought and ponder rationalistically, touching remote things—things that only theoretically matter, such as the transit of Venus. But only at their peril can men rationalize about so practical a matter as health.

XI Science and the Savages

A permanent disadvantage of the study of folk-lore and kindred subjects is that the man of science can hardly be in the nature of things very frequently a man of the world. He is a student of nature; he is scarcely ever a student of human nature. And even where this difficulty is overcome, and he is in some sense a student of human nature, this is only a very faint beginning of the painful progress towards being human. For the study of primitive race and religion stands apart in one important respect from all, or nearly all, the ordinary scientific studies. A man can understand astronomy only by being an astronomer; he can understand entomology only by being an entomologist (or, perhaps, an insect); but he can understand a great deal of anthropology merely by being a man. He is himself the animal which he studies. Hence arises the fact which strikes the eye everywhere in the records of ethnology and folk-lore—the fact that the same frigid and detached spirit which leads to success in the study of astronomy or botany leads to disaster in the study of mythology or human origins. It is necessary to cease to be a man in order to do justice to a microbe; it is not necessary to cease to be a man in order to do justice to men. That same suppression of sympathies, that same waving away of intuitions or guess-work which make a man preternaturally clever in dealing with the stomach of a spider, will make him preternaturally stupid in dealing with the heart of man. He is making himself inhuman in order to understand humanity. An ignorance of the other world is boasted by many men of science; but in this matter their defect arises, not from ignorance of the other world, but from ignorance of this world. For the secrets about which anthropologists concern themselves can be best learnt, not from books or voyages, but from the ordinary commerce of man with man. The secret of why some savage tribe worships monkeys or the moon is not to be found even by travelling among those savages and taking down their answers in a note-book, although the cleverest man may pursue this course.

The answer to the riddle is in England; it is in London; nay, it is in his own heart. When a man has discovered why men in Bond Street wear black hats he will at the same moment have discovered why men in Timbuctoo wear red feathers. The mystery in the heart of some savage war-dance should not be studied in books of scientific travel; it should be studied at a subscription ball. If a man desires to find out the origins of religions, let him not go to the Sandwich Islands; let him go to church. If a man wishes to know the origin of human society, to know what society, philosophically speaking, really is, let him not go into the British Museum; let him go into society.

This total misunderstanding of the real nature of ceremonial gives rise to the most awkward and dehumanized versions of the conduct of men in rude lands or ages. The man of science, not realizing that ceremonial is essentially a thing which is done without a reason, has to find a reason for every sort of ceremonial, and, as might be supposed, the reason is generally a very absurd one—absurd because it originates not in the simple mind of the barbarian, but in the sophisticated mind of the professor. The teamed man will say, for instance, "The natives of Mumbojumbo Land believe that the dead man can eat and will require food upon his journey to the other world. This is attested by the fact that they place food in the grave, and that any family not complying with this rite is the object of the anger of the priests and the tribe." To any one acquainted with humanity this way of talking is topsy-turvy. It is like saying, "The English in the twentieth century believed that a dead man could smell. This is attested by the fact that they always covered his grave with lilies, violets, or other flowers. Some priestly and tribal terrors were evidently attached to the neglect of this action, as we have records of several old ladies who were very much disturbed in mind because their wreaths had not arrived in time for the funeral." It may be of course that savages put food with a dead man because they think that a dead man can eat, or weapons with a dead man because they think that a dead man can fight. But personally I do not believe that they think anything of the kind. I believe they put food or weapons on the dead for the same reason that we put flowers, because it is an exceedingly natural and obvious thing to do. We do not understand, it is true, the emotion which makes us think it obvious and natural; but that is because, like all the important emotions of human existence it is essentially irrational. We do not understand the savage for the same reason that the savage does not understand himself. And the savage does not understand himself for the same reason that we do not understand ourselves either.

The obvious truth is that the moment any matter has passed through the human mind it is finally and for ever spoilt for all purposes of science. It has become a thing incurably mysterious and infinite; this mortal has put on immortality. Even what we call our material desires are spiritual, because they are human. Science can analyse a pork-chop, and say how much of it is phosphorus and how much is protein; but science cannot analyse any man's wish for a pork-chop, and say how much of it is hunger, how much custom, how much nervous fancy, how much a haunting love of the beautiful. The man's desire for the pork-chop remains literally as mystical and ethereal as his desire for heaven. All attempts, therefore, at a science of any human things, at a science of history, a science of folk-lore, a science of sociology, are by their nature not merely hopeless, but crazy. You can no more be certain in economic history that a man's desire for money was merely a desire for money than you can be certain in hagiology that a saint's desire for God was merely a desire for God. And this kind of vagueness in the primary phenomena of the study is an absolutely final blow to anything in the nature of a science. Men can construct a science with very few instruments, or with very plain instruments; but no one on earth could construct a science with unreliable instruments. A man might work out the whole of mathematics with a handful of pebbles, but not with a handful of clay which was always falling apart into new fragments, and falling together into new combinations. A man might measure heaven and earth with a reed, but not with a growing reed.

As one of the enormous follies of folk-lore, let us take the case of the transmigration of stories, and the alleged unity of their source. Story after story the scientific mythologists have cut out of its place in history, and pinned side by side with similar stories in their museum of fables. The process is industrious, it is fascinating, and the whole of it rests on one of the plainest fallacies in the world. That a story has been told all over the place at some time or other, not only does not prove that it never really happened; it does not even faintly indicate or make slightly more probable that it never happened. That a large number of fishermen have falsely asserted that they have caught a pike two feet long, does not in the least affect the question of whether any one ever really did so. That numberless journalists announce a Franco-German war merely for money is no evidence one way or the other upon the dark question of whether such a war ever occurred. Doubtless in a few hundred years the innumerable Franco-German wars that did not happen will have cleared the scientific mind of any belief in the legendary war of '70 which did. But that will be because if folk-lore students remain at all, their nature will be unchanged; and their services to folk-lore will be still as they are at present, greater than they know. For in truth these men do something far more godlike than studying legends; they create them.

There are two kinds of stories which the scientists say cannot be true, because everybody tells them. The first class consists of the stories which are told everywhere, because they are somewhat odd or clever; there is nothing in the world to prevent their having happened to somebody as an adventure any more than there is anything to prevent their having occurred, as they certainly did occur, to somebody as an idea. But they are not likely to have happened to many people. The second class of their "myths" consist of the stories that are told everywhere for the simple reason that they happen everywhere. Of the first class, for instance, we might take such an example as the story of William Tell, now generally ranked among legends upon the sole ground that it is found in the tales of other peoples. Now, it is obvious that this was told everywhere because whether true or fictitious it is what is called "a good story;" it is odd, exciting, and it has a climax. But to suggest that some such eccentric incident can never have happened in the whole history of archery, or that it did not happen to any particular person of whom it is told, is stark impudence. The idea of shooting at a mark attached to some valuable or beloved person is an idea doubtless that might easily have occurred to any inventive poet. But it is also an idea that might easily occur to any boastful archer. It might be one of the fantastic caprices of some story-teller. It might equally well be one of the fantastic caprices of some tyrant. It might occur first in real life and afterwards occur in legends. Or it might just as well occur first in legends and afterwards occur in real life. If no apple has ever been shot off a boy's head from the beginning of the world, it may be done tomorrow morning, and by somebody who has never heard of William Tell.

This type of tale, indeed, may be pretty fairly paralleled with the ordinary anecdote terminating in a repartee or an Irish bull. Such a retort as the famous "je ne vois pas la necessite" we have all seen attributed to Talleyrand, to Voltaire, to Henri Quatre, to an anonymous judge, and so on. But this variety does not in any way make it more likely that the thing was never said at all. It is highly likely that it was really said by somebody unknown. It is highly likely that it was really said by Talleyrand. In any case, it is not any more difficult to believe that the mot might have occurred to a man in conversation than to a man writing memoirs. It might have occurred to any of the men I have mentioned. But there is this point of distinction about it, that it is not likely to have occurred to all of them. And this is where the first class of so-called myth differs from the second to which I have previously referred. For there is a second class of incident found to be common to the stories of five or six heroes, say to Sigurd, to Hercules, to Rustem, to the Cid, and so on. And the peculiarity of this myth is that not only is it highly reasonable to imagine that it really happened to one hero, but it is highly reasonable to imagine that it really happened to all of them. Such a story, for instance, is that of a great man having his strength swayed or thwarted by the mysterious weakness of a woman. The anecdotal story, the story of William Tell, is as I have said, popular, because it is peculiar. But this kind of story, the story of Samson and Delilah of Arthur and Guinevere, is obviously popular because it is not peculiar. It is popular as good, quiet fiction is popular, because it tells the truth about people. If the ruin of Samson by a woman, and the ruin of Hercules by a woman, have a common legendary origin, it is gratifying to know that we can also explain, as a fable, the ruin of Nelson by a woman and the ruin of Parnell by a woman. And, indeed, I have no doubt whatever that, some centuries hence, the students of folk-lore will refuse altogether to believe that Elizabeth Barrett eloped with Robert Browning, and will prove their point up to the hilt by the unquestionable fact that the whole fiction of the period was full of such elopements from end to end.

Possibly the most pathetic of all the delusions of the modern students of primitive belief is the notion they have about the thing they call anthropomorphism. They believe that primitive men attributed phenomena to a god in human form in order to explain them, because his mind in its sullen limitation could not reach any further than his own clownish existence. The thunder was called the voice of a man, the lightning the eyes of a man, because by this explanation they were made more reasonable and comfortable. The final cure for all this kind of philosophy is to walk down a lane at night. Any one who does so will discover very quickly that men pictured something semi-human at the back of all things, not because such a thought was natural, but because it was supernatural; not because it made things more comprehensible, but because it made them a hundred times more incomprehensible and mysterious. For a man walking down a lane at night can see the conspicuous fact that as long as nature keeps to her own course, she has no power with us at all. As long as a tree is a tree, it is a top-heavy monster with a hundred arms, a thousand tongues, and only one leg. But so long as a tree is a tree, it does not frighten us at all. It begins to be something alien, to be something strange, only when it looks like ourselves. When a tree really looks like a man our knees knock under us. And when the whole universe looks like a man we fall on our faces.

XII Paganism and Mr. Lowes Dickinson

Of the New Paganism (or neo-Paganism), as it was preached flamboyantly by Mr. Swinburne or delicately by Walter Pater, there is no necessity to take any very grave account, except as a thing which left behind it incomparable exercises in the English language. The New Paganism is no longer new, and it never at any time bore the smallest resemblance to Paganism. The ideas about the ancient civilization which it has left loose in the public mind are certainly extraordinary enough. The term "pagan" is continually used in fiction and light literature as meaning a man without any religion, whereas a pagan was generally a man with about half a dozen. The pagans, according to this notion, were continually crowning themselves with flowers and dancing about in an irresponsible state, whereas, if there were two things that the best pagan civilization did honestly believe in, they were a rather too rigid dignity and a much too rigid responsibility. Pagans are depicted as above all things inebriate and lawless, whereas they were above all things reasonable and respectable. They are praised as disobedient when they had only one great virtue—civic obedience. They are envied and admired as shamelessly happy when they had only one great sin—despair.

Mr. Lowes Dickinson, the most pregnant and provocative of recent writers on this and similar subjects, is far too solid a man to have fallen into this old error of the mere anarchy of Paganism. In order to make hay of that Hellenic enthusiasm which has as its ideal mere appetite and egotism, it is not necessary to know much philosophy, but merely to know a little Greek. Mr. Lowes Dickinson knows a great deal of philosophy, and also a great deal of Greek, and his error, if error he has, is not that of the crude hedonist. But the contrast which he offers between Christianity and Paganism in the matter of moral ideals—a contrast which he states very ably in a paper called "How long halt ye?" which appeared in the Independent Review—does, I think, contain an error of a deeper kind. According to him, the ideal of Paganism was not, indeed, a mere frenzy of lust and liberty and caprice, but was an ideal of full and satisfied humanity. According to him, the ideal of Christianity was the ideal of asceticism. When I say that I think this idea wholly wrong as a matter of philosophy and history, I am not talking for the moment about any ideal Christianity of my own, or even of any primitive Christianity undefiled by after events. I am not, like so many modern Christian idealists, basing my case upon certain things which Christ said. Neither am I, like so many other Christian idealists, basing my case upon certain things that Christ forgot to say. I take historic Christianity with all its sins upon its head; I take it, as I would take Jacobinism, or Mormonism, or any other mixed or unpleasing human product, and I say that the meaning of its action was not to be found in asceticism. I say that its point of departure from Paganism was not asceticism. I say that its point of difference with the modern world was not asceticism. I say that St. Simeon Stylites had not his main inspiration in asceticism. I say that the main Christian impulse cannot be described as asceticism, even in the ascetics.

Let me set about making the matter clear. There is one broad fact about the relations of Christianity and Paganism which is so simple that many will smile at it, but which is so important that all moderns forget it. The primary fact about Christianity and Paganism is that one came after the other. Mr. Lowes Dickinson speaks of them as if they were parallel ideals—even speaks as if Paganism were the newer of the two, and the more fitted for a new age. He suggests that the Pagan ideal will be the ultimate good of man; but if that is so, we must at least ask with more curiosity than he allows for, why it was that man actually found his ultimate good on earth under the stars, and threw it away again. It is this extraordinary enigma to which I propose to attempt an answer.

There is only one thing in the modern world that has been face to face with Paganism; there is only one thing in the modern world which in that sense knows anything about Paganism: and that is Christianity. That fact is really the weak point in the whole of that hedonistic neo-Paganism of which I have spoken. All that genuinely remains of the ancient hymns or the ancient dances of Europe, all that has honestly come to us from the festivals of Phoebus or Pan, is to be found in the festivals of the Christian Church. If any one wants to hold the end of a chain which really goes back to the heathen mysteries, he had better take hold of a festoon of flowers at Easter or a string of sausages at Christmas. Everything else in the modern world is of Christian origin, even everything that seems most anti-Christian. The French Revolution is of Christian origin. The newspaper is of Christian origin. The anarchists are of Christian origin. Physical science is of Christian origin. The attack on Christianity is of Christian origin. There is one thing, and one thing only, in existence at the present day which can in any sense accurately be said to be of pagan origin, and that is Christianity.

The real difference between Paganism and Christianity is perfectly summed up in the difference between the pagan, or natural, virtues, and those three virtues of Christianity which the Church of Rome calls virtues of grace. The pagan, or rational, virtues are such things as justice and temperance, and Christianity has adopted them. The three mystical virtues which Christianity has not adopted, but invented, are faith, hope, and charity. Now much easy and foolish Christian rhetoric could easily be poured out upon those three words, but I desire to confine myself to the two facts which are evident about them. The first evident fact (in marked contrast to the delusion of the dancing pagan)—the first evident fact, I say, is that the pagan virtues, such as justice and temperance, are the sad virtues, and that the mystical virtues of faith, hope, and charity are the gay and exuberant virtues. And the second evident fact, which is even more evident, is the fact that the pagan virtues are the reasonable virtues, and that the Christian virtues of faith, hope, and charity are in their essence as unreasonable as they can be.

As the word "unreasonable" is open to misunderstanding, the matter may be more accurately put by saying that each one of these Christian or mystical virtues involves a paradox in its own nature, and that this is not true of any of the typically pagan or rationalist virtues. Justice consists in finding out a certain thing due to a certain man and giving it to him. Temperance consists in finding out the proper limit of a particular indulgence and adhering to that. But charity means pardoning what is unpardonable, or it is no virtue at all. Hope means hoping when things are hopeless, or it is no virtue at all. And faith means believing the incredible, or it is no virtue at all.

It is somewhat amusing, indeed, to notice the difference between the fate of these three paradoxes in the fashion of the modern mind. Charity is a fashionable virtue in our time; it is lit up by the gigantic firelight of Dickens. Hope is a fashionable virtue to-day; our attention has been arrested for it by the sudden and silver trumpet of Stevenson. But faith is unfashionable, and it is customary on every side to cast against it the fact that it is a paradox. Everybody mockingly repeats the famous childish definition that faith is "the power of believing that which we know to be untrue." Yet it is not one atom more paradoxical than hope or charity. Charity is the power of defending that which we know to be indefensible. Hope is the power of being cheerful in circumstances which we know to be desperate. It is true that there is a state of hope which belongs to bright prospects and the morning; but that is not the virtue of hope. The virtue of hope exists only in earthquake and, eclipse. It is true that there is a thing crudely called charity, which means charity to the deserving poor; but charity to the deserving is not charity at all, but justice. It is the undeserving who require it, and the ideal either does not exist at all, or exists wholly for them. For practical purposes it is at the hopeless moment that we require the hopeful man, and the virtue either does not exist at all, or begins to exist at that moment. Exactly at the instant when hope ceases to be reasonable it begins to be useful. Now the old pagan world went perfectly straightforward until it discovered that going straightforward is an enormous mistake. It was nobly and beautifully reasonable, and discovered in its death-pang this lasting and valuable truth, a heritage for the ages, that reasonableness will not do. The pagan age was truly an Eden or golden age, in this essential sense, that it is not to be recovered. And it is not to be recovered in this sense again that, while we are certainly jollier than the pagans, and much more right than the pagans, there is not one of us who can, by the utmost stretch of energy, be so sensible as the pagans. That naked innocence of the intellect cannot be recovered by any man after Christianity; and for this excellent reason, that every man after Christianity knows it to be misleading. Let me take an example, the first that occurs to the mind, of this impossible plainness in the pagan point of view. The greatest tribute to Christianity in the modern world is Tennyson's "Ulysses." The poet reads into the story of Ulysses the conception of an incurable desire to wander. But the real Ulysses does not desire to wander at all. He desires to get home. He displays his heroic and unconquerable qualities in resisting the misfortunes which baulk him; but that is all. There is no love of adventure for its own sake; that is a Christian product. There is no love of Penelope for her own sake; that is a Christian product. Everything in that old world would appear to have been clean and obvious. A good man was a good man; a bad man was a bad man. For this reason they had no charity; for charity is a reverent agnosticism towards the complexity of the soul. For this reason they had no such thing as the art of fiction, the novel; for the novel is a creation of the mystical idea of charity. For them a pleasant landscape was pleasant, and an unpleasant landscape unpleasant. Hence they had no idea of romance; for romance consists in thinking a thing more delightful because it is dangerous; it is a Christian idea. In a word, we cannot reconstruct or even imagine the beautiful and astonishing pagan world. It was a world in which common sense was really common.

My general meaning touching the three virtues of which I have spoken will now, I hope, be sufficiently clear. They are all three paradoxical, they are all three practical, and they are all three paradoxical because they are practical. it is the stress of ultimate need, and a terrible knowledge of things as they are, which led men to set up these riddles, and to die for them. Whatever may be the meaning of the contradiction, it is the fact that the only kind of hope that is of any use in a battle is a hope that denies arithmetic. Whatever may be the meaning of the contradiction, it is the fact that the only kind of charity which any weak spirit wants, or which any generous spirit feels, is the charity which forgives the sins that are like scarlet. Whatever may be the meaning of faith, it must always mean a certainty about something we cannot prove. Thus, for instance, we believe by faith in the existence of other people.

But there is another Christian virtue, a virtue far more obviously and historically connected with Christianity, which will illustrate even better the connection between paradox and practical necessity. This virtue cannot be questioned in its capacity as a historical symbol; certainly Mr. Lowes Dickinson will not question it. It has been the boast of hundreds of the champions of Christianity. It has been the taunt of hundreds of the opponents of Christianity. It is, in essence, the basis of Mr. Lowes Dickinson's whole distinction between Christianity and Paganism. I mean, of course, the virtue of humility. I admit, of course, most readily, that a great deal of false Eastern humility (that is, of strictly ascetic humility) mixed itself with the main stream of European Christianity. We must not forget that when we speak of Christianity we are speaking of a whole continent for about a thousand years. But of this virtue even more than of the other three, I would maintain the general proposition adopted above.

Civilization discovered Christian humility for the same urgent reason that it discovered faith and charity—that is, because Christian civilization had to discover it or die.

The great psychological discovery of Paganism, which turned it into Christianity, can be expressed with some accuracy in one phrase. The pagan set out, with admirable sense, to enjoy himself. By the end of his civilization he had discovered that a man cannot enjoy himself and continue to enjoy anything else. Mr. Lowes Dickinson has pointed out in words too excellent to need any further elucidation, the absurd shallowness of those who imagine that the pagan enjoyed himself only in a materialistic sense. Of course, he enjoyed himself, not only intellectually even, he enjoyed himself morally, he enjoyed himself spiritually. But it was himself that he was enjoying; on the face of it, a very natural thing to do. Now, the psychological discovery is merely this, that whereas it had been supposed that the fullest possible enjoyment is to be found by extending our ego to infinity, the truth is that the fullest possible enjoyment is to be found by reducing our ego to zero.

Humility is the thing which is for ever renewing the earth and the stars. It is humility, and not duty, which preserves the stars from wrong, from the unpardonable wrong of casual resignation; it is through humility that the most ancient heavens for us are fresh and strong. The curse that came before history has laid on us all a tendency to be weary of wonders. If we saw the sun for the first time it would be the most fearful and beautiful of meteors. Now that we see it for the hundredth time we call it, in the hideous and blasphemous phrase of Wordsworth, "the light of common day." We are inclined to increase our claims. We are inclined to demand six suns, to demand a blue sun, to demand a green sun. Humility is perpetually putting us back in the primal darkness. There all light is lightning, startling and instantaneous. Until we understand that original dark, in which we have neither sight nor expectation, we can give no hearty and childlike praise to the splendid sensationalism of things. The terms "pessimism" and "optimism," like most modern terms, are unmeaning. But if they can be used in any vague sense as meaning something, we may say that in this great fact pessimism is the very basis of optimism. The man who destroys himself creates the universe. To the humble man, and to the humble man alone, the sun is really a sun; to the humble man, and to the humble man alone, the sea is really a sea. When he looks at all the faces in the street, he does not only realize that men are alive, he realizes with a dramatic pleasure that they are not dead.

I have not spoken of another aspect of the discovery of humility as a psychological necessity, because it is more commonly insisted on, and is in itself more obvious. But it is equally clear that humility is a permanent necessity as a condition of effort and self-examination. It is one of the deadly fallacies of Jingo politics that a nation is stronger for despising other nations. As a matter of fact, the strongest nations are those, like Prussia or Japan, which began from very mean beginnings, but have not been too proud to sit at the feet of the foreigner and learn everything from him. Almost every obvious and direct victory has been the victory of the plagiarist. This is, indeed, only a very paltry by-product of humility, but it is a product of humility, and, therefore, it is successful. Prussia had no Christian humility in its internal arrangements; hence its internal arrangements were miserable. But it had enough Christian humility slavishly to copy France (even down to Frederick the Great's poetry), and that which it had the humility to copy it had ultimately the honour to conquer. The case of the Japanese is even more obvious; their only Christian and their only beautiful quality is that they have humbled themselves to be exalted. All this aspect of humility, however, as connected with the matter of effort and striving for a standard set above us, I dismiss as having been sufficiently pointed out by almost all idealistic writers.

It may be worth while, however, to point out the interesting disparity in the matter of humility between the modern notion of the strong man and the actual records of strong men. Carlyle objected to the statement that no man could be a hero to his valet. Every sympathy can be extended towards him in the matter if he merely or mainly meant that the phrase was a disparagement of hero-worship. Hero-worship is certainly a generous and human impulse; the hero may be faulty, but the worship can hardly be. It may be that no man would be a hero to his valet. But any man would be a valet to his hero. But in truth both the proverb itself and Carlyle's stricture upon it ignore the most essential matter at issue. The ultimate psychological truth is not that no man is a hero to his valet. The ultimate psychological truth, the foundation of Christianity, is that no man is a hero to himself. Cromwell, according to Carlyle, was a strong man. According to Cromwell, he was a weak one.

The weak point in the whole of Carlyle's case for aristocracy lies, indeed, in his most celebrated phrase. Carlyle said that men were mostly fools. Christianity, with a surer and more reverent realism, says that they are all fools. This doctrine is sometimes called the doctrine of original sin. It may also be described as the doctrine of the equality of men. But the essential point of it is merely this, that whatever primary and far-reaching moral dangers affect any man, affect all men. All men can be criminals, if tempted; all men can be heroes, if inspired. And this doctrine does away altogether with Carlyle's pathetic belief (or any one else's pathetic belief) in "the wise few." There are no wise few. Every aristocracy that has ever existed has behaved, in all essential points, exactly like a small mob. Every oligarchy is merely a knot of men in the street —that is to say, it is very jolly, but not infallible. And no oligarchies in the world's history have ever come off so badly in practical affairs as the very proud oligarchies—the oligarchy of Poland, the oligarchy of Venice. And the armies that have most swiftly and suddenly broken their enemies in pieces have been the religious armies—the Moslem Armies, for instance, or the Puritan Armies. And a religious army may, by its nature, be defined as an army in which every man is taught not to exalt but to abase himself. Many modern Englishmen talk of themselves as the sturdy descendants of their sturdy Puritan fathers. As a fact, they would run away from a cow. If you asked one of their Puritan fathers, if you asked Bunyan, for instance, whether he was sturdy, he would have answered, with tears, that he was as weak as water. And because of this he would have borne tortures. And this virtue of humility, while being practical enough to win battles, will always be paradoxical enough to puzzle pedants. It is at one with the virtue of charity in this respect. Every generous person will admit that the one kind of sin which charity should cover is the sin which is inexcusable. And every generous person will equally agree that the one kind of pride which is wholly damnable is the pride of the man who has something to be proud of. The pride which, proportionally speaking, does not hurt the character, is the pride in things which reflect no credit on the person at all. Thus it does a man no harm to be proud of his country, and comparatively little harm to be proud of his remote ancestors. It does him more harm to be proud of having made money, because in that he has a little more reason for pride. It does him more harm still to be proud of what is nobler than money—intellect. And it does him most harm of all to value himself for the most valuable thing on earth—goodness. The man who is proud of what is really creditable to him is the Pharisee, the man whom Christ Himself could not forbear to strike.

My objection to Mr. Lowes Dickinson and the reassertors of the pagan ideal is, then, this. I accuse them of ignoring definite human discoveries in the moral world, discoveries as definite, though not as material, as the discovery of the circulation of the blood. We cannot go back to an ideal of reason and sanity. For mankind has discovered that reason does not lead to sanity. We cannot go back to an ideal of pride and enjoyment. For mankind has discovered that pride does not lead to enjoyment. I do not know by what extraordinary mental accident modern writers so constantly connect the idea of progress with the idea of independent thinking. Progress is obviously the antithesis of independent thinking. For under independent or individualistic thinking, every man starts at the beginning, and goes, in all probability, just as far as his father before him. But if there really be anything of the nature of progress, it must mean, above all things, the careful study and assumption of the whole of the past. I accuse Mr. Lowes Dickinson and his school of reaction in the only real sense. If he likes, let him ignore these great historic mysteries—the mystery of charity, the mystery of chivalry, the mystery of faith. If he likes, let him ignore the plough or the printing-press. But if we do revive and pursue the pagan ideal of a simple and rational self-completion we shall end—where Paganism ended. I do not mean that we shall end in destruction. I mean that we shall end in Christianity.

XIII. Celts and Celtophiles

Science in the modern world has many uses; its chief use, however, is to provide long words to cover the errors of the rich. The word "kleptomania" is a vulgar example of what I mean. It is on a par with that strange theory, always advanced when a wealthy or prominent person is in the dock, that exposure is more of a punishment for the rich than for the poor. Of course, the very reverse is the truth. Exposure is more of a punishment for the poor than for the rich. The richer a man is the easier it is for him to be a tramp. The richer a man is the easier it is for him to be popular and generally respected in the Cannibal Islands. But the poorer a man is the more likely it is that he will have to use his past life whenever he wants to get a bed for the night. Honour is a luxury for aristocrats, but it is a necessity for hall-porters. This is a secondary matter, but it is an example of the general proposition I offer—the proposition that an enormous amount of modern ingenuity is expended on finding defences for the indefensible conduct of the powerful. As I have said above, these defences generally exhibit themselves most emphatically in the form of appeals to physical science. And of all the forms in which science, or pseudo-science, has come to the rescue of the rich and stupid, there is none so singular as the singular invention of the theory of races.

When a wealthy nation like the English discovers the perfectly patent fact that it is making a ludicrous mess of the government of a poorer nation like the Irish, it pauses for a moment in consternation, and then begins to talk about Celts and Teutons. As far as I can understand the theory, the Irish are Celts and the English are Teutons. Of course, the Irish are not Celts any more than the English are Teutons. I have not followed the ethnological discussion with much energy, but the last scientific conclusion which I read inclined on the whole to the summary that the English were mainly Celtic and the Irish mainly Teutonic. But no man alive, with even the glimmering of a real scientific sense, would ever dream of applying the terms "Celtic" or "Teutonic" to either of them in any positive or useful sense.

That sort of thing must be left to people who talk about the Anglo-Saxon race, and extend the expression to America. How much of the blood of the Angles and Saxons (whoever they were) there remains in our mixed British, Roman, German, Dane, Norman, and Picard stock is a matter only interesting to wild antiquaries. And how much of that diluted blood can possibly remain in that roaring whirlpool of America into which a cataract of Swedes, Jews, Germans, Irishmen, and Italians is perpetually pouring, is a matter only interesting to lunatics. It would have been wiser for the English governing class to have called upon some other god. All other gods, however weak and warring, at least boast of being constant. But science boasts of being in a flux for ever; boasts of being unstable as water.

And England and the English governing class never did call on this absurd deity of race until it seemed, for an instant, that they had no other god to call on. All the most genuine Englishmen in history would have yawned or laughed in your face if you had begun to talk about Anglo-Saxons. If you had attempted to substitute the ideal of race for the ideal of nationality, I really do not like to think what they would have said. I certainly should not like to have been the officer of Nelson who suddenly discovered his French blood on the eve of Trafalgar. I should not like to have been the Norfolk or Suffolk gentleman who had to expound to Admiral Blake by what demonstrable ties of genealogy he was irrevocably bound to the Dutch. The truth of the whole matter is very simple. Nationality exists, and has nothing in the world to do with race. Nationality is a thing like a church or a secret society; it is a product of the human soul and will; it is a spiritual product. And there are men in the modern world who would think anything and do anything rather than admit that anything could be a spiritual product.

A nation, however, as it confronts the modern world, is a purely spiritual product. Sometimes it has been born in independence, like Scotland. Sometimes it has been born in dependence, in subjugation, like Ireland. Sometimes it is a large thing cohering out of many smaller things, like Italy. Sometimes it is a small thing breaking away from larger things, like Poland. But in each and every case its quality is purely spiritual, or, if you will, purely psychological. It is a moment when five men become a sixth man. Every one knows it who has ever founded a club. It is a moment when five places become one place. Every one must know it who has ever had to repel an invasion. Mr. Timothy Healy, the most serious intellect in the present House of Commons, summed up nationality to perfection when he simply called it something for which people will die, As he excellently said in reply to Lord Hugh Cecil, "No one, not even the noble lord, would die for the meridian of Greenwich." And that is the great tribute to its purely psychological character. It is idle to ask why Greenwich should not cohere in this spiritual manner while Athens or Sparta did. It is like asking why a man falls in love with one woman and not with another.

Now, of this great spiritual coherence, independent of external circumstances, or of race, or of any obvious physical thing, Ireland is the most remarkable example. Rome conquered nations, but Ireland has conquered races. The Norman has gone there and become Irish, the Scotchman has gone there and become Irish, the Spaniard has gone there and become Irish, even the bitter soldier of Cromwell has gone there and become Irish. Ireland, which did not exist even politically, has been stronger than all the races that existed scientifically. The purest Germanic blood, the purest Norman blood, the purest blood of the passionate Scotch patriot, has not been so attractive as a nation without a flag. Ireland, unrecognized and oppressed, has easily absorbed races, as such trifles are easily absorbed. She has easily disposed of physical science, as such superstitions are easily disposed of. Nationality in its weakness has been stronger than ethnology in its strength. Five triumphant races have been absorbed, have been defeated by a defeated nationality.

This being the true and strange glory of Ireland, it is impossible to hear without impatience of the attempt so constantly made among her modern sympathizers to talk about Celts and Celticism. Who were the Celts? I defy anybody to say. Who are the Irish? I defy any one to be indifferent, or to pretend not to know. Mr. W. B. Yeats, the great Irish genius who has appeared in our time, shows his own admirable penetration in discarding altogether the argument from a Celtic race. But he does not wholly escape, and his followers hardly ever escape, the general objection to the Celtic argument. The tendency of that argument is to represent the Irish or the Celts as a strange and separate race, as a tribe of eccentrics in the modern world immersed in dim legends and fruitless dreams. Its tendency is to exhibit the Irish as odd, because they see the fairies. Its trend is to make the Irish seem weird and wild because they sing old songs and join in strange dances. But this is quite an error; indeed, it is the opposite of the truth. It is the English who are odd because they do not see the fairies. It is the inhabitants of Kensington who are weird and wild because they do not sing old songs and join in strange dances. In all this the Irish are not in the least strange and separate, are not in the least Celtic, as the word is commonly and popularly used. In all this the Irish are simply an ordinary sensible nation, living the life of any other ordinary and sensible nation which has not been either sodden with smoke or oppressed by money-lenders, or otherwise corrupted with wealth and science. There is nothing Celtic about having legends. It is merely human. The Germans, who are (I suppose) Teutonic, have hundreds of legends, wherever it happens that the Germans are human. There is nothing Celtic about loving poetry; the English loved poetry more, perhaps, than any other people before they came under the shadow of the chimney-pot and the shadow of the chimney-pot hat. It is not

Ireland which is mad and mystic; it is Manchester which is mad and mystic, which is incredible, which is a wild exception among human things. Ireland has no need to play the silly game of the science of races; Ireland has no need to pretend to be a tribe of visionaries apart. In the matter of visions, Ireland is more than a nation, it is a model nation.

XIV On Certain Modern Writers and the Institution of the Family

The family may fairly be considered, one would think, an ultimate human institution. Every one would admit that it has been the main cell and central unit of almost all societies hitherto, except, indeed, such societies as that of Lacedaemon, which went in for "efficiency," and has, therefore, perished, and left not a trace behind. Christianity, even enormous as was its revolution, did not alter this ancient and savage sanctity; it merely reversed it. It did not deny the trinity of father, mother, and child. It merely read it backwards, making it run child, mother, father. This it called, not the family, but the Holy Family, for many things are made holy by being turned upside down. But some sages of our own decadence have made a serious attack on the family. They have impugned it, as I think wrongly; and its defenders have defended it, and defended it wrongly. The common defence of the family is that, amid the stress and fickleness of life, it is peaceful, pleasant, and at one. But there is another defence of the family which is possible, and to me evident; this defence is that the family is not peaceful and not pleasant and not at one.

It is not fashionable to say much nowadays of the advantages of the small community. We are told that we must go in for large empires and large ideas. There is one advantage, however, in the small state, the city, or the village, which only the wilfully blind can overlook. The man who lives in a small community lives in a much larger world. He knows much more of the fierce varieties and uncompromising divergences of men. The reason is obvious. In a large community we can choose our companions. In a small community our companions are chosen for us. Thus in all extensive and highly civilized societies groups come into existence founded upon what is called sympathy, and shut out the real world more sharply than the gates of a monastery. There is nothing really narrow about the clan; the thing which is really narrow is the clique. The men of the clan live together because they all wear the same tartan or are all descended from the same sacred cow; but in their souls, by the divine luck of things, there will always be more colours than in any tartan. But the men of the clique live together because they have the same kind of soul, and their narrowness is a narrowness of spiritual coherence and contentment, like that which exists in hell. A big society exists in order to form cliques. A big society is a society for the promotion of narrowness. It is a machinery for the purpose of guarding the solitary and sensitive individual from all experience of the bitter and bracing human compromises. It is, in the most literal sense of the words, a society for the prevention of Christian knowledge.

We can see this change, for instance, in the modern transformation of the thing called a club. When London was smaller, and the parts of London more self-contained and parochial, the club was what it still is in villages, the opposite of what it is now in great cities. Then the club was valued as a place where a man could be sociable. Now the club is valued as a place where a man can be unsociable. The more the enlargement and elaboration of our civilization goes on the more the club ceases to be a place where a man can have a noisy argument, and becomes more and more a place where a man can have what is somewhat fantastically called a quiet chop. Its aim is to make a man comfortable, and to make a man comfortable is to make him the opposite of sociable. Sociability, like all good things, is full of discomforts, dangers, and renunciations. The club tends to produce the most degraded of all combinations—the luxurious anchorite, the man who combines the self-indulgence of Lucullus with the insane loneliness of St. Simeon Stylites.

If we were to-morrow morning snowed up in the street in which we live, we should step suddenly into a much larger and much wilder world than we have ever known. And it is the whole effort of the typically modern person to escape from the street in which he lives. First he invents modern hygiene and goes to Margate.

Then he invents modern culture and goes to Florence. Then he invents modern imperialism and goes to Timbuctoo. He goes to the fantastic borders of the earth. He pretends to shoot tigers. He almost rides on a camel. And in all this he is still essentially fleeing from the street in which he was born; and of this flight he is always ready with his own explanation. He says he is fleeing from his street because it is dull; he is lying. He is really fleeing from his street because it is a great deal too exciting. It is exciting because it is exacting; it is exacting because it is alive. He can visit Venice because to him the Venetians are only Venetians; the people in his own street are men. He can stare at the Chinese because for him the Chinese are a passive thing to be stared at; if he stares at the old lady in the next garden, she becomes active. He is forced to flee, in short, from the too stimulating society of his equals—of free men, perverse, personal, deliberately different from himself. The street in Brixton is too glowing and overpowering. He has to soothe and quiet himself among tigers and vultures, camels and crocodiles. These creatures are indeed very different from himself. But they do not put their shape or colour or custom into a decisive intellectual competition with his own. They do not seek to destroy his principles and assert their own; the stranger monsters of the suburban street do seek to do this. The camel does not contort his features into a fine sneer because Mr. Robinson has not got a hump; the cultured gentleman at No. 5 does exhibit a sneer because Robinson has not got a dado. The vulture will not roar with laughter because a man does not fly; but the major at No. 9 will roar with laughter because a man does not smoke. The complaint we commonly have to make of our neighbours is that they will not, as we express it, mind their own business. We do not really mean that they will not mind their own business. If our neighbours did not mind their own business they would be asked abruptly for their rent, and would rapidly cease to be our neighbours. What we really mean when we say that they cannot mind their own business is something much deeper. We do not dislike them because they have so little force and fire that they cannot be interested in themselves. We dislike them because they have so much force and fire that they can be interested in us as well. What we dread about our neighbours, in short, is not the narrowness of their horizon, but their superb tendency to broaden it. And all aversions to ordinary humanity have this general character. They are not aversions to its feebleness (as is pretended), but to its energy. The misanthropes pretend that they despise humanity for its weakness. As a matter of fact, they hate it for its strength.

Of course, this shrinking from the brutal vivacity and brutal variety of common men is a perfectly reasonable and excusable thing as long as it does not pretend to any point of superiority. It is when it calls itself aristocracy or aestheticism or a superiority to the bourgeoisie that its inherent weakness has in justice to be pointed out. Fastidiousness is the most pardonable of vices; but it is the most unpardonable of virtues. Nietzsche, who represents most prominently this pretentious claim of the fastidious, has a description somewhere—a very powerful description in the purely literary sense—of the disgust and disdain which consume him at the sight of the common people with their common faces, their common voices, and their common minds. As I have said, this attitude is almost beautiful if we may regard it as pathetic. Nietzsche's aristocracy has about it all the sacredness that belongs to the weak. When he makes us feel that he cannot endure the innumerable faces, the incessant voices, the overpowering omnipresence which belongs to the mob, he will have the sympathy of anybody who has ever been sick on a steamer or tired in a crowded omnibus. Every man has hated mankind when he was less than a man. Every man has had humanity in his eyes like a blinding fog, humanity in his nostrils like a suffocating smell. But when Nietzsche has the incredible lack of humour and lack of imagination to ask us to believe that his aristocracy is an aristocracy of strong muscles or an aristocracy of strong wills, it is necessary to point out the truth. It is an aristocracy of weak nerves.

We make our friends; we make our enemies; but God makes our next-door neighbour. Hence he comes to us clad in all the careless terrors of nature; he is as strange as the stars, as reckless and indifferent as the rain. He is Man, the most terrible of the beasts. That is why the old religions and the old scriptural language showed so sharp a wisdom when they spoke, not of one's duty towards humanity, but one's duty towards one's neighbour. The duty towards humanity may often take the form of some choice which is personal or even pleasurable. That duty may be a hobby; it may even be a dissipation. We may work in the East End because we are peculiarly fitted to work in the East End, or because we think we are; we may fight for the cause of international peace because we are very fond of fighting. The most monstrous martyrdom, the most repulsive experience, may be the result of choice or a kind of taste. We may be so made as to be particularly fond of lunatics or specially interested in leprosy. We may love negroes because they are black or German Socialists because they are pedantic. But we have to love our neighbour because he is there—a much more alarming reason for a much more serious operation. He is the sample of humanity which is actually given us. Precisely because he may be anybody he is everybody. He is a symbol because he is an accident.

Doubtless men flee from small environments into lands that are very deadly. But this is natural enough; for they are not fleeing from death. They are fleeing from life. And this principle applies to ring within ring of the social system of humanity. It is perfectly reasonable that men should seek for some particular variety of the human type, so long as they are seeking for that variety of the human type, and not for mere human variety. It is quite proper that a British diplomatist should seek the society of Japanese generals, if what he wants is Japanese generals. But if what he wants is people different from himself, he had much better stop at home and discuss religion with the housemaid. It is quite reasonable that the village genius should come up to conquer London if what he wants is to conquer London. But if he wants to conquer something fundamentally and symbolically hostile and also very strong, he had much better remain where he is and have a row with the rector. The man in the suburban street is quite right if he goes to Ramsgate for the sake of Ramsgate—a difficult thing to imagine. But if, as he expresses it, he goes to Ramsgate "for a change," then he would have a much more romantic and even melodramatic change if he jumped over the wall into his neighbours garden. The consequences would be bracing in a sense far beyond the possibilities of Ramsgate hygiene.

Now, exactly as this principle applies to the empire, to the nation within the empire, to the city within the nation, to the street within the city, so it applies to the home within the street. The institution of the family is to be commended for precisely the same reasons that the institution of the nation, or the institution of the city, are in this matter to be commended. It is a good thing for a man to live in a family for the same reason that it is a good thing for a man to be besieged in a city. It is a good thing for a man to live in a family in the same sense that it is a beautiful and delightful thing for a man to be snowed up in a street. They all force him to realize that life is not a thing from outside, but a thing from inside. Above all, they all insist upon the fact that life, if it be a truly stimulating and fascinating life, is a thing which, of its nature, exists in spite of ourselves. The modern writers who have suggested, in a more or less open manner, that the family is a bad institution, have generally confined themselves to suggesting, with much sharpness, bitterness, or pathos, that perhaps the family is not always very congenial. Of course the family is a good institution because it is uncongenial. It is wholesome precisely because it contains so many divergencies and varieties. It is, as the sentimentalists say, like a little kingdom, and, like most other little kingdoms, is generally in a state of something resembling anarchy. It is exactly because our brother George is not interested in our religious difficulties, but is interested in the Trocadero Restaurant, that the family has some of the bracing qualities of the commonwealth. It is precisely because our uncle Henry does not approve of the theatrical ambitions of our sister Sarah that the family is like humanity. The men and women who, for good reasons and bad, revolt against the family, are, for good reasons and bad, simply revolting against mankind. Aunt Elizabeth is unreasonable, like mankind. Papa is excitable, like mankind Our youngest brother is mischievous, like mankind. Grandpapa is stupid, like the world; he is old, like the world.

Those who wish, rightly or wrongly, to step out of all this, do definitely wish to step into a narrower world. They are dismayed and terrified by the largeness and variety of the family. Sarah wishes to find a world wholly consisting of private theatricals; George wishes to think the Trocadero a cosmos. I do not say, for a moment, that the flight to this narrower life may not be the right thing for the individual, any more than I say the same thing about flight into a monastery. But I do say that anything is bad and artificial which tends to make these people succumb to the strange delusion that they are stepping into a world which is actually larger and more varied than their own. The best way that a man could test his readiness to encounter the common variety of mankind would be to climb down a chimney into any house at random, and get on as well as possible with the people inside. And that is essentially what each one of us did on the day that he was born.

This is, indeed, the sublime and special romance of the family. It is romantic because it is a toss-up. It is romantic because it is everything that its enemies call it. It is romantic because it is arbitrary. It is romantic because it is there. So long as you have groups of men chosen rationally, you have some special or sectarian atmosphere. It is when you have groups of men chosen irrationally that you have men. The element of adventure begins to exist; for an adventure is, by its nature, a thing that comes to us. It is a thing that chooses us, not a thing that we choose. Falling in love has been often regarded as the supreme adventure, the supreme romantic accident. In so much as there is in it something outside ourselves, something of a sort of merry fatalism, this is very true. Love does take us and transfigure and torture us. It does break our hearts with an unbearable beauty, like the unbearable beauty of music. But in so far as we have certainly something to do with the matter; in so far as we are in some sense prepared to fall in love and in some sense jump into it; in so far as we do to some extent choose and to some extent even judge—in all this falling in love is not truly romantic, is not truly adventurous at all. In this degree the supreme adventure is not falling in love. The supreme adventure is being born. There we do walk suddenly into a splendid and startling trap. There we do see something of which we have not dreamed before. Our father and mother do lie in wait for us and leap out on us, like brigands from a bush. Our uncle is a surprise. Our aunt is, in the beautiful common expression, a bolt from the blue. When we step into the family, by the act of being born, we do step into a world which is incalculable, into a world which has its own strange laws, into a world which could do without us, into a world that we have not made. In other words, when we step into the family we step into a fairy-tale.

This colour as of a fantastic narrative ought to cling to the family and to our relations with it throughout life. Romance is the deepest thing in life; romance is deeper even than reality. For even if reality could be proved to be misleading, it still could not be proved to be unimportant or unimpressive. Even if the facts are false, they are still very strange. And this strangeness of life, this unexpected and even perverse element of things as they fall out, remains incurably interesting. The circumstances we can regulate may become tame or pessimistic; but the "circumstances over which we have no control" remain god-like to those who, like Mr. Micawber, can call on them and renew their strength. People wonder why the novel is the most popular form of literature; people wonder why it is read more than books of science or books of metaphysics. The reason is very simple; it is merely that the novel is more true than they are. Life may sometimes legitimately appear as a book of science. Life may sometimes appear, and with a much greater legitimacy, as a book of metaphysics. But life is always a novel. Our existence may cease to be a song; it may cease even to be a beautiful lament. Our existence may not be an intelligible justice, or even a recognizable wrong. But our existence is still a story. In the fiery alphabet of every sunset is written, "to be continued in our next." If we have sufficient intellect, we can finish a philosophical and exact deduction, and be certain that we are finishing it right. With the adequate brain-power we could finish any scientific discovery, and be certain that we were finishing it right. But not with the most gigantic intellect could we finish the simplest or silliest story, and be certain that we were finishing it right. That is because a story has behind it, not merely intellect which is partly mechanical, but will, which is in its essence divine. The narrative writer can send his hero to the gallows if he likes in the last chapter but one. He can do it by the same divine caprice whereby he, the author, can go to the gallows himself, and to hell afterwards if he chooses. And the same civilization, the chivalric European civilization which asserted freewill in the thirteenth century, produced the thing called "fiction" in the eighteenth. When Thomas Aquinas asserted the spiritual liberty of man, he created all the bad novels in the circulating libraries.

But in order that life should be a story or romance to us, it is necessary that a great part of it, at any rate, should be settled for us without our permission. If we wish life to be a system, this may be a nuisance; but if we wish it to be a drama, it is an essential. It may often happen, no doubt, that a drama may be written by somebody else which we like very little. But we should like it still less if the author came before the curtain every hour or so, and forced on us the whole trouble of inventing the next act. A man has control over many things in his life; he has control over enough things to be the hero of a novel. But if he had control over everything, there would be so much hero that there would be no novel. And the reason why the lives of the rich are at bottom so tame and uneventful is simply that they can choose the events. They are dull because they are omnipotent. They fail to feel adventures because they can make the adventures. The thing which keeps life romantic and full of fiery possibilities is the existence of these great plain limitations which force all of us to meet the things we do not like or do not expect. It is vain for the supercilious moderns to talk of being in uncongenial surroundings. To be in a romance is to be in uncongenial surroundings. To be born into this earth is to be born into uncongenial surroundings, hence to be born into a romance. Of all these great limitations and frameworks which fashion and create the poetry and variety of life, the family is the most definite and important. Hence it is misunderstood by the moderns, who imagine that romance would exist most perfectly in a complete state of what they call liberty. They think that if a man makes a gesture it would be a startling and romantic matter that the sun should fall from the sky. But the startling and romantic thing about the sun is that it does not fall from the sky. They are seeking under every shape and form a world where there are no limitations—that is, a world where there are no outlines; that is, a world where there are no shapes. There is nothing baser than that infinity. They say they wish to be, as strong as the universe, but they really wish the whole universe as weak as themselves.

XV On Smart Novelists and the Smart Set

In one sense, at any rate, it is more valuable to read bad literature than good literature. Good literature may tell us the mind of one man; but bad literature may tell us the mind of many men. A good novel tells us the truth about its hero; but a bad novel tells us the truth about its author. It does much more than that, it tells us the truth about its readers; and, oddly enough, it tells us this all the more the more cynical and immoral be the motive of its manufacture. The more dishonest a book is as a book the more honest it is as a public document. A sincere novel exhibits the simplicity of one particular man; an insincere novel exhibits the simplicity of mankind. The pedantic decisions and definable readjustments of man may be found in scrolls and statute books and scriptures; but men's basic assumptions and everlasting energies are to be found in penny dreadfuls and halfpenny novelettes. Thus a man, like many men of real culture in our day, might learn from good literature nothing except the power to appreciate good literature. But from bad literature he might learn to govern empires and look over the map of mankind.

There is one rather interesting example of this state of things in which the weaker literature is really the stronger and the stronger the weaker. It is the case of what may be called, for the sake of an approximate description, the literature of aristocracy; or, if you prefer the description, the literature of snobbishness. Now if any one wishes to find a really effective and comprehensible and permanent case for aristocracy well and sincerely stated, let him read, not the modern philosophical conservatives, not even Nietzsche, let him read the Bow Bells Novelettes. Of the case of Nietzsche I am confessedly more doubtful. Nietzsche and the Bow Bells Novelettes have both obviously the same fundamental character; they both worship the tall man with curling moustaches and herculean bodily power, and they both worship him in a manner which is somewhat feminine and hysterical. Even here, however, the Novelette easily maintains its philosophical superiority, because it does attribute to the strong man those virtues which do commonly belong to him, such virtues as laziness and kindliness and a rather reckless benevolence, and a great dislike of hurting the weak. Nietzsche, on the other hand, attributes to the strong man that scorn against weakness which only exists among invalids. It is not, however, of the secondary merits of the great German philosopher, but of the primary merits of the Bow Bells Novelettes, that it is my present affair to speak. The picture of aristocracy in the popular sentimental novelette seems to me very satisfactory as a permanent political and philosophical guide. It may be inaccurate about details such as the title by which a baronet is addressed or the width of a mountain chasm which a baronet can conveniently leap, but it is not a bad description of the general idea and intention of aristocracy as they exist in human affairs. The essential dream of aristocracy is magnificence and valour; and if the Family Herald Supplement sometimes distorts or exaggerates these things, at least, it does not fall short in them. It never errs by making the mountain chasm too narrow or the title of the baronet insufficiently impressive. But above this sane reliable old literature of snobbishness there has arisen in our time another kind of literature of snobbishness which, with its much higher pretensions, seems to me worthy of very much less respect. Incidentally (if that matters), it is much better literature. But it is immeasurably worse philosophy, immeasurably worse ethics and politics, immeasurably worse vital rendering of aristocracy and humanity as they really are. From such books as those of which I wish now to speak we can discover what a clever man can do with the idea of aristocracy. But from the Family Herald Supplement literature we can learn what the idea of aristocracy can do with a man who is not clever. And when we know that we know English history.

This new aristocratic fiction must have caught the attention of everybody who has read the best fiction for the last fifteen years.

It is that genuine or alleged literature of the Smart Set which represents that set as distinguished, not only by smart dresses, but by smart sayings. To the bad baronet, to the good baronet, to the romantic and misunderstood baronet who is supposed to be a bad baronet, but is a good baronet, this school has added a conception undreamed of in the former years—the conception of an amusing baronet. The aristocrat is not merely to be taller than mortal men and stronger and handsomer, he is also to be more witty. He is the long man with the short epigram. Many eminent, and deservedly eminent, modern novelists must accept some responsibility for having supported this worst form of snobbishness—an intellectual snobbishness. The talented author of "Dodo" is responsible for having in some sense created the fashion as a fashion. Mr. Hichens, in the "Green Carnation," reaffirmed the strange idea that young noblemen talk well; though his case had some vague biographical foundation, and in consequence an excuse. Mrs. Craigie is considerably guilty in the matter, although, or rather because, she has combined the aristocratic note with a note of some moral and even religious sincerity. When you are saving a man's soul, even in a novel, it is indecent to mention that he is a gentleman. Nor can blame in this matter be altogether removed from a man of much greater ability, and a man who has proved his possession of the highest of human instinct, the romantic instinct—I mean Mr. Anthony Hope. In a galloping, impossible melodrama like "The Prisoner of Zenda," the blood of kings fanned an excellent fantastic thread or theme. But the blood of kings is not a thing that can be taken seriously. And when, for example, Mr. Hope devotes so much serious and sympathetic study to the man called Tristram of Blent, a man who throughout burning boyhood thought of nothing but a silly old estate, we feel even in Mr. Hope the hint of this excessive concern about the oligarchic idea. It is hard for any ordinary person to feel so much interest in a young man whose whole aim is to own the house of Blent at the time when every other young man is owning the stars.

Mr. Hope, however, is a very mild case, and in him there is not only an element of romance, but also a fine element of irony which warns us against taking all this elegance too seriously. Above all, he shows his sense in not making his noblemen so incredibly equipped with impromptu repartee. This habit of insisting on the wit of the wealthier classes is the last and most servile of all the servilities. It is, as I have said, immeasurably more contemptible than the snobbishness of the novelette which describes the nobleman as smiling like an Apollo or riding a mad elephant. These may be exaggerations of beauty and courage, but beauty and courage are the unconscious ideals of aristocrats, even of stupid aristocrats.

The nobleman of the novelette may not be sketched with any very close or conscientious attention to the daily habits of noblemen. But he is something more important than a reality; he is a practical ideal. The gentleman of fiction may not copy the gentleman of real life; but the gentleman of real life is copying the gentleman of fiction. He may not be particularly good-looking, but he would rather be good-looking than anything else; he may not have ridden on a mad elephant, but he rides a pony as far as possible with an air as if he had. And, upon the whole, the upper class not only especially desire these qualities of beauty and courage, but in some degree, at any rate, especially possess them. Thus there is nothing really mean or sycophantic about the popular literature which makes all its marquises seven feet high. It is snobbish, but it is not servile. Its exaggeration is based on an exuberant and honest admiration; its honest admiration is based upon something which is in some degree, at any rate, really there. The English lower classes do not fear the English upper classes in the least; nobody could. They simply and freely and sentimentally worship them. The strength of the aristocracy is not in the aristocracy at all; it is in the slums. It is not in the House of Lords; it is not in the Civil Service; it is not in the Government offices; it is not even in the huge and disproportionate monopoly of the

English land. It is in a certain spirit. It is in the fact that when a navvy wishes to praise a man, it comes readily to his tongue to say that he has behaved like a gentleman. From a democratic point of view he might as well say that he had behaved like a viscount. The oligarchic character of the modern English commonwealth does not rest, like many oligarchies, on the cruelty of the rich to the poor. It does not even rest on the kindness of the rich to the poor. It rests on the perennial and unfailing kindness of the poor to the rich.

The snobbishness of bad literature, then, is not servile; but the snobbishness of good literature is servile. The old-fashioned halfpenny romance where the duchesses sparkled with diamonds was not servile; but the new romance where they sparkle with epigrams is servile. For in thus attributing a special and startling degree of intellect and conversational or controversial power to the upper classes, we are attributing something which is not especially their virtue or even especially their aim. We are, in the words of Disraeli (who, being a genius and not a gentleman, has perhaps primarily to answer for the introduction of this method of flattering the gentry), we are performing the essential function of flattery which is flattering the people for the qualities they have not got. Praise may be gigantic and insane without having any quality of flattery so long as it is praise of something that is noticeably in existence. A man may say that a giraffe's head strikes the stars, or that a whale fills the German Ocean, and still be only in a rather excited state about a favourite animal. But when he begins to congratulate the giraffe on his feathers, and the whale on the elegance of his legs, we find ourselves confronted with that social element which we call flattery. The middle and lower orders of London can sincerely, though not perhaps safely, admire the health and grace of the English aristocracy. And this for the very simple reason that the aristocrats are, upon the whole, more healthy and graceful than the poor. But they cannot honestly admire the wit of the aristocrats. And this for the simple reason that the aristocrats are not more witty than the poor, but a very great deal less so. A man does not hear, as in the smart novels, these gems of verbal felicity dropped between diplomatists at dinner. Where he really does hear them is between two omnibus conductors in a block in Holborn. The witty peer whose impromptus fill the books of Mrs. Craigie or Miss Fowler, would, as a matter of fact, be torn to shreds in the art of conversation by the first boot-black he had the misfortune to fall foul of. The poor are merely sentimental, and very excusably sentimental, if they praise the gentleman for having a ready hand and ready money. But they are strictly slaves and sycophants if they praise him for having a ready tongue. For that they have far more themselves.

The element of oligarchical sentiment in these novels, however, has, I think, another and subtler aspect, an aspect more difficult to understand and more worth understanding. The modern gentleman, particularly the modern English gentleman, has become so central and important in these books, and through them in the whole of our current literature and our current mode of thought, that certain qualities of his, whether original or recent, essential or accidental, have altered the quality of our English comedy. In particular, that stoical ideal, absurdly supposed to be the English ideal, has stiffened and chilled us. It is not the English ideal; but it is to some extent the aristocratic ideal; or it may be only the ideal of aristocracy in its autumn or decay. The gentleman is a Stoic because he is a sort of savage, because he is filled with a great elemental fear that some stranger will speak to him. That is why a third-class carriage is a community, while a first-class carriage is a place of wild hermits. But this matter, which is difficult, I may be permitted to approach in a more circuitous way.

The haunting element of ineffectualness which runs through so much of the witty and epigrammatic fiction fashionable during the last eight or ten years, which runs through such works of a real though varying ingenuity as "Dodo," or "Concerning Isabel

Carnaby," or even "Some Emotions and a Moral," may be expressed in various ways, but to most of us I think it will ultimately amount to the same thing. This new frivolity is inadequate because there is in it no strong sense of an unuttered joy. The men and women who exchange the repartees may not only be hating each other, but hating even themselves. Any one of them might be bankrupt that day, or sentenced to be shot the next. They are joking, not because they are merry, but because they are not; out of the emptiness of the heart the mouth speaketh. Even when they talk pure nonsense it is a careful nonsense—a nonsense of which they are economical, or, to use the perfect expression of Mr. W. S. Gilbert in "Patience," it is such "precious nonsense." Even when they become light-headed they do not become light-hearted. All those who have read anything of the rationalism of the moderns know that their Reason is a sad thing. But even their unreason is sad.

The causes of this incapacity are also not very difficult to indicate. The chief of all, of course, is that miserable fear of being sentimental, which is the meanest of all the modern terrors—meaner even than the terror which produces hygiene. Everywhere the robust and uproarious humour has come from the men who were capable not merely of sentimentalism, but a very silly sentimentalism. There has been no humour so robust or uproarious as that of the sentimentalist Steele or the sentimentalist Sterne or the sentimentalist Dickens. These creatures who wept like women were the creatures who laughed like men. It is true that the humour of Micawber is good literature and that the pathos of little Nell is bad. But the kind of man who had the courage to write so badly in the one case is the kind of man who would have the courage to write so well in the other. The same unconsciousness, the same violent innocence, the same gigantesque scale of action which brought the Napoleon of Comedy his Jena brought him also his Moscow. And herein is especially shown the frigid and feeble limitations of our modern wits. They make violent efforts, they make heroic and almost pathetic efforts, but they cannot really write badly. There are moments when we almost think that they are achieving the effect, but our hope shrivels to nothing the moment we compare their little failures with the enormous imbecilities of Byron or Shakespeare.

For a hearty laugh it is necessary to have touched the heart. I do not know why touching the heart should always be connected only with the idea of touching it to compassion or a sense of distress. The heart can be touched to joy and triumph; the heart can be touched to amusement. But all our comedians are tragic comedians. These later fashionable writers are so pessimistic in bone and marrow that they never seem able to imagine the heart having any concern with mirth. When they speak of the heart, they always mean the pangs and disappointments of the emotional life. When they say that a man's heart is in the right place, they mean, apparently, that it is in his boots. Our ethical societies understand fellowship, but they do not understand good fellowship. Similarly, our wits understand talk, but not what Dr. Johnson called a good talk. In order to have, like Dr. Johnson, a good talk, it is emphatically necessary to be, like Dr. Johnson, a good man—to have friendship and honour and an abysmal tenderness. Above all, it is necessary to be openly and indecently humane, to confess with fulness all the primary pities and fears of Adam. Johnson was a clear-headed humorous man, and therefore he did not mind talking seriously about religion. Johnson was a brave man, one of the bravest that ever walked, and therefore he did not mind avowing to any one his consuming fear of death.

The idea that there is something English in the repression of one's feelings is one of those ideas which no Englishman ever heard of until England began to be governed exclusively by Scotchmen, Americans, and Jews. At the best, the idea is a generalization from the Duke of Wellington—who was an Irishman. At the worst, it is a part of that silly Teutonism which knows as little about England as it does about anthropology, but which is always talking about Vikings. As a matter of fact, the Vikings did not repress their feelings in the least. They cried like babies and kissed each other like girls; in short, they acted in that respect like Achilles and all strong heroes the children of the gods. And though the English nationality has probably not much more to do with the Vikings than the French nationality or the Irish nationality, the English have certainly been the children of the Vikings in the matter of tears and kisses. It is not merely true that all the most typically English men of letters, like Shakespeare and Dickens, Richardson and Thackeray, were sentimentalists. It is also true that all the most typically English men of action were sentimentalists, if possible, more sentimental. In the great Elizabethan age, when the English nation was finally hammered out, in the great eighteenth century when the British Empire was being built up everywhere, where in all these times, where was this symbolic stoical Englishman who dresses in drab and black and represses his feelings? Were all the Elizabethan palladins and pirates like that? Were any of them like that? Was Grenville concealing his emotions when he broke wine-glasses to pieces with his teeth and bit them till the blood poured down? Was Essex restraining his excitement when he threw his hat into the sea? Did Raleigh think it sensible to answer the Spanish guns only, as Stevenson says, with a flourish of insulting trumpets? Did Sydney ever miss an opportunity of making a theatrical remark in the whole course of his life and death? Were even the Puritans Stoics? The English Puritans repressed a good deal, but even they were too English to repress their feelings. It was by a great miracle of genius assuredly that Carlyle contrived to admire simultaneously two things so irreconcilably opposed as silence and Oliver Cromwell. Cromwell was the very reverse of a strong, silent man. Cromwell was always talking, when he was not crying. Nobody, I suppose, will accuse the author of "Grace Abounding" of being ashamed of his feelings. Milton, indeed, it might be possible to represent as a Stoic; in some sense he was a Stoic, just as he was a prig and a polygamist and several other unpleasant and heathen things. But when we have passed that great and desolate name, which may really be counted an exception, we find the tradition of English emotionalism immediately resumed and unbrokenly continuous. Whatever may have been the moral beauty of the passions of Etheridge and Dorset, Sedley and Buckingham, they cannot be accused of the fault of fastidiously concealing them. Charles the Second was very popular with the English because, like all the jolly English kings, he displayed his passions. William the Dutchman was very unpopular with the English because, not being an Englishman, he did hide his emotions. He was, in fact, precisely the ideal Englishman of our modern theory; and precisely for that reason all the real Englishmen loathed him like leprosy. With the rise of the great England of the eighteenth century, we find this open and emotional tone still maintained in letters and politics, in arts and in arms. Perhaps the only quality which was possessed in common by the great Fielding, and the great Richardson was that neither of them hid their feelings. Swift, indeed, was hard and logical, because Swift was Irish. And when we pass to the soldiers and the rulers, the patriots and the empire-builders of the eighteenth century, we find, as I have said, that they were, If possible, more romantic than the romancers, more poetical than the poets. Chatham, who showed the world all his strength, showed the House of Commons all his weakness. Wolfe walked about the room with a drawn sword calling himself Caesar and Hannibal, and went to death with poetry in his mouth. Clive was a man of the same type as Cromwell or Bunyan, or, for the matter of that, Johnson—that is, he was a strong, sensible man with a kind of running spring of hysteria and melancholy in him. Like Johnson, he was all the more healthy because he was morbid. The tales of all the admirals and adventurers of that England are full of braggadocio, of sentimentality, of splendid affectation. But it is scarcely necessary to multiply examples of the essentially romantic Englishman when one example towers above them all. Mr. Rudyard Kipling has said complacently of the

English, "We do not fall on the neck and kiss when we come together." It is true that this ancient and universal custom has vanished with the modern weakening of England. Sydney would have thought nothing of kissing Spenser. But I willingly concede that Mr. Broderick would not be likely to kiss Mr. Arnold-Foster, if that be any proof of the increased manliness and military greatness of England. But the Englishman who does not show his feelings has not altogether given up the power of seeing something English in the great sea-hero of the Napoleonic war. You cannot break the legend of Nelson. And across the sunset of that glory is written in flaming letters for ever the great English sentiment, "Kiss me, Hardy."

This ideal of self-repression, then, is, whatever else it is, not English. It is, perhaps, somewhat Oriental, it is slightly Prussian, but in the main it does not come, I think, from any racial or national source. It is, as I have said, in some sense aristocratic; it comes not from a people, but from a class. Even aristocracy, I think, was not quite so stoical in the days when it was really strong. But whether this unemotional ideal be the genuine tradition of the gentleman, or only one of the inventions of the modern gentleman (who may be called the decayed gentleman), it certainly has something to do with the unemotional quality in these society novels. From representing aristocrats as people who suppressed their feelings, it has been an easy step to representing aristocrats as people who had no feelings to suppress. Thus the modern oligarchist has made a virtue for the oligarchy of the hardness as well as the brightness of the diamond. Like a sonneteer addressing his lady in the seventeenth century, he seems to use the word "cold" almost as a eulogium, and the word "heartless" as a kind of compliment. Of course, in people so incurably kind-hearted and babyish as are the English gentry, it would be impossible to create anything that can be called positive cruelty; so in these books they exhibit a sort of negative cruelty. They cannot be cruel in acts, but they can be so in words. All this means one thing, and one thing only. It means that the living and invigorating ideal of England must be looked for in the masses; it must be looked for where Dickens found it—Dickens among whose glories it was to be a humorist, to be a sentimentalist, to be an optimist, to be a poor man, to be an Englishman, but the greatest of whose glories was that he saw all mankind in its amazing and tropical luxuriance, and did not even notice the aristocracy; Dickens, the greatest of whose glories was that he could not describe a gentleman.

XVI On Mr. McCabe and a Divine Frivolity

A critic once remonstrated with me saying, with an air of indignant reasonableness, "If you must make jokes, at least you need not make them on such serious subjects." I replied with a natural simplicity and wonder, "About what other subjects can one make jokes except serious subjects?" It is quite useless to talk about profane jesting. All jesting is in its nature profane, in the sense that it must be the sudden realization that something which thinks itself solemn is not so very solemn after all. If a joke is not a joke about religion or morals, it is a joke about police-magistrates or scientific professors or undergraduates dressed up as Queen Victoria. And people joke about the police-magistrate more than they joke about the Pope, not because the police-magistrate is a more frivolous subject, but, on the contrary, because the police-magistrate is a more serious subject than the Pope. The Bishop of Rome has no jurisdiction in this realm of England; whereas the police-magistrate may bring his solemnity to bear quite suddenly upon us. Men make jokes about old scientific professors, even more than they make them about bishops—not because science is lighter than religion, but because science is always by its nature more solemn and austere than religion. It is not I; it is not even a particular class of journalists or jesters who make jokes about the matters which are of most awful import; it is the whole human race. If there is one thing more than another which any one will admit who has the smallest knowledge of the world, it is that men are always speaking gravely and earnestly and with the utmost possible care about the things that are not important, but always talking frivolously about the things that are. Men talk for hours with the faces of a college of cardinals about things like golf, or tobacco, or waistcoats, or party politics. But all the most grave and dreadful things in the world are the oldest jokes in the world—being married; being hanged.

One gentleman, however, Mr. McCabe, has in this matter made to me something that almost amounts to a personal appeal; and as he happens to be a man for whose sincerity and intellectual virtue I have a high respect, I do not feel inclined to let it pass without some attempt to satisfy my critic in the matter. Mr. McCabe devotes a considerable part of the last essay in the collection called "Christianity and Rationalism on Trial" to an objection, not to my thesis, but to my method, and a very friendly and dignified appeal to me to alter it. I am much inclined to defend myself in this matter out of mere respect for Mr. McCabe, and still more so out of mere respect for the truth which is, I think, in danger by his error, not only in this question, but in others. In order that there may be no injustice done in the matter, I will quote Mr. McCabe himself. "But before I follow Mr. Chesterton in some detail I would make a general observation on his method. He is as serious as I am in his ultimate purpose, and I respect him for that. He knows, as I do, that humanity stands at a solemn parting of the ways. Towards some unknown goal it presses through the ages, impelled by an overmastering desire of happiness. To-day it hesitates, lightheartedly enough, but every serious thinker knows how momentous the decision may be. It is, apparently, deserting the path of religion and entering upon the path of secularism. Will it lose itself in quagmires of sensuality down this new path, and pant and toil through years of civic and industrial anarchy, only to learn it had lost the road, and must return to religion? Or will it find that at last it is leaving the mists and the quagmires behind it; that it is ascending the slope of the hill so long dimly discerned ahead, and making straight for the long-sought Utopia? This is the drama of our time, and every man and every woman should understand it.

"Mr. Chesterton understands it. Further, he gives us credit for understanding it. He has nothing of that paltry meanness or strange density of so many of his colleagues, who put us down as aimless iconoclasts or moral anarchists. He admits that we are waging a thankless war for what we take to be Truth and Progress. He is doing the same. But why, in the name of all that is reasonable, should we, when we are agreed on the momentousness of the issue either way, forthwith desert serious methods of conducting the controversy? Why, when the vital need of our time is to induce men and women to collect their thoughts occasionally, and be men and women—nay, to remember that they are really gods that hold the destinies of humanity on their knees—why should we think that this kaleidoscopic play of phrases is inopportune? The ballets of the Alhambra, and the fireworks of the Crystal Palace, and Mr. Chesterton's Daily News articles, have their place in life. But how a serious social student can think of curing the thoughtlessness of our generation by strained paradoxes; of giving people a sane grasp of social problems by literary sleight-of-hand; of settling important questions by a reckless shower of rocket-metaphors and inaccurate 'facts,' and the substitution of imagination for judgment, I cannot see."

I quote this passage with a particular pleasure, because Mr. McCabe certainly cannot put too strongly the degree to which I give him and his school credit for their complete sincerity and responsibility of philosophical attitude. I am quite certain that they mean every word they say. I also mean every word I say. But why is it that Mr. McCabe has some sort of mysterious hesitation about admitting that I mean every word I say; why is it that he is not quite as certain of my mental responsibility as I am of his mental responsibility? If we attempt to answer the question directly and well, we shall, I think, have come to the root of the matter by the shortest cut.

Mr. McCabe thinks that I am not serious but only funny, because Mr. McCabe thinks that funny is the opposite of serious. Funny is the opposite of not funny, and of nothing else. The question of whether a man expresses himself in a grotesque or laughable phraseology, or in a stately and restrained phraseology, is not a question of motive or of moral state, it is a question of instinctive language and self-expression. Whether a man chooses to tell the truth in long sentences or short jokes is a problem analogous to whether he chooses to tell the truth in French or German. Whether a man preaches his gospel grotesquely or gravely is merely like the question of whether he preaches it in prose or verse. The question of whether Swift was funny in his irony is quite another sort of question to the question of whether Swift was serious in his pessimism. Surely even Mr. McCabe would not maintain that the more funny "Gulliver" is in its method the less it can be sincere in its object. The truth is, as I have said, that in this sense the two qualities of fun and seriousness have nothing whatever to do with each other, they are no more comparable than black and triangular. Mr. Bernard Shaw is funny and sincere. Mr. George Robey is funny and not sincere. Mr. McCabe is sincere and not funny. The average Cabinet Minister is not sincere and not funny.

In short, Mr. McCabe is under the influence of a primary fallacy which I have found very common in men of the clerical type. Numbers of clergymen have from time to time reproached me for making jokes about religion; and they have almost always invoked the authority of that very sensible commandment which says, "Thou shalt not take the name of the Lord thy God in vain." Of course, I pointed out that I was not in any conceivable sense taking the name in vain. To take a thing and make a joke out of it is not to take it in vain. It is, on the contrary, to take it and use it for an uncommonly good object. To use a thing in vain means to use it without use. But a joke may be exceedingly useful; it may contain the whole earthly sense, not to mention the whole heavenly sense, of a situation. And those who find in the Bible the commandment can find in the Bible any number of the jokes. In the same book in which God's name is fenced from being taken in vain, God himself overwhelms Job with a torrent of terrible levities. The same book which says that God's name must not be taken vainly, talks easily and carelessly about God laughing and

God winking. Evidently it is not here that we have to look for genuine examples of what is meant by a vain use of the name. And it is not very difficult to see where we have really to look for it. The people (as I tactfully pointed out to them) who really take the name of the Lord in vain are the clergymen themselves. The thing which is fundamentally and really frivolous is not a careless joke. The thing which is fundamentally and really frivolous is a careless solemnity. If Mr. McCabe really wishes to know what sort of guarantee of reality and solidity is afforded by the mere act of what is called talking seriously, let him spend a happy Sunday in going the round of the pulpits. Or, better still, let him drop in at the House of Commons or the House of Lords. Even Mr. McCabe would admit that these men are solemn—more solemn than I am. And even Mr. McCabe, I think, would admit that these men are frivolous—more frivolous than I am. Why should Mr. McCabe be so eloquent about the danger arising from fantastic and paradoxical writers? Why should he be so ardent in desiring grave and verbose writers? There are not so very many fantastic and paradoxical writers. But there are a gigantic number of grave and verbose writers; and it is by the efforts of the grave and verbose writers that everything that Mr. McCabe detests (and everything that I detest, for that matter) is kept in existence and energy. How can it have come about that a man as intelligent as Mr. McCabe can think that paradox and jesting stop the way? It is solemnity that is stopping the way in every department of modern effort. It is his own favourite "serious methods;" it is his own favourite "momentousness;" it is his own favourite "judgment" which stops the way everywhere. Every man who has ever headed a deputation to a minister knows this. Every man who has ever written a letter to the Times knows it. Every rich man who wishes to stop the mouths of the poor talks about "momentousness." Every Cabinet minister who has not got an answer suddenly develops a "judgment." Every sweater who uses vile methods recommends "serious methods." I said a moment ago that sincerity had nothing to do with solemnity, but I confess that I am not so certain that I was right. In the modern world, at any rate, I am not so sure that I was right. In the modern world solemnity is the direct enemy of sincerity. In the modern world sincerity is almost always on one side, and solemnity almost always on the other. The only answer possible to the fierce and glad attack of sincerity is the miserable answer of solemnity. Let Mr. McCabe, or any one else who is much concerned that we should be grave in order to be sincere, simply imagine the scene in some government office in which Mr. Bernard Shaw should head a Socialist deputation to Mr. Austen Chamberlain. On which side would be the solemnity? And on which the sincerity?

I am, indeed, delighted to discover that Mr. McCabe reckons Mr. Shaw along with me in his system of condemnation of frivolity. He said once, I believe, that he always wanted Mr. Shaw to label his paragraphs serious or comic. I do not know which paragraphs of Mr. Shaw are paragraphs to be labelled serious; but surely there can be no doubt that this paragraph of Mr. McCabe's is one to be labelled comic. He also says, in the article I am now discussing, that Mr. Shaw has the reputation of deliberately saying everything which his hearers do not expect him to say. I need not labour the inconclusiveness and weakness of this, because it has already been dealt with in my remarks on Mr. Bernard Shaw. Suffice it to say here that the only serious reason which I can imagine inducing any one person to listen to any other is, that the first person looks to the second person with an ardent faith and a fixed attention, expecting him to say what he does not expect him to say. It may be a paradox, but that is because paradoxes are true. It may not be rational, but that is because rationalism is wrong. But clearly it is quite true that whenever we go to hear a prophet or teacher we may or may not expect wit, we may or may not expect eloquence, but we do expect what we do not expect. We may not expect the true, we may not even expect the wise, but we do expect the unexpected. If we do not expect the unexpected, why do we go there at all? If we expect the expected, why do we not sit at home and expect it by ourselves? If Mr. McCabe means merely this about Mr. Shaw, that he always has some unexpected application of his doctrine to give to those who listen to him, what he says is quite true, and to say it is only to say that Mr. Shaw is an original man. But if he means that Mr. Shaw has ever professed or preached any doctrine but one, and that his own, then what he says is not true. It is not my business to defend Mr. Shaw; as has been seen already, I disagree with him altogether. But I do not mind, on his behalf offering in this matter a flat defiance to all his ordinary opponents, such as Mr. McCabe. I defy Mr. McCabe, or anybody else, to mention one single instance in which Mr. Shaw has, for the sake of wit or novelty, taken up any position which was not directly deducible from the body of his doctrine as elsewhere expressed. I have been, I am happy to say, a tolerably close student of Mr. Shaw's utterances, and I request Mr. McCabe, if he will not believe that I mean anything else, to believe that I mean this challenge.

All this, however, is a parenthesis. The thing with which I am here immediately concerned is Mr. McCabe's appeal to me not to be so frivolous. Let me return to the actual text of that appeal. There are, of course, a great many things that I might say about it in detail. But I may start with saying that Mr. McCabe is in error in supposing that the danger which I anticipate from the disappearance of religion is the increase of sensuality. On the contrary, I should be inclined to anticipate a decrease in sensuality, because I anticipate a decrease in life. I do not think that under modern Western materialism we should have anarchy. I doubt whether we should have enough individual valour and spirit even to have liberty. It is quite an old-fashioned fallacy to suppose that our objection to scepticism is that it removes the discipline from life. Our objection to scepticism is that it removes the motive power. Materialism is not a thing which destroys mere restraint. Materialism itself is the great restraint. The McCabe school advocates a political liberty, but it denies spiritual liberty.

That is, it abolishes the laws which could be broken, and substitutes laws that cannot. And that is the real slavery.

The truth is that the scientific civilization in which Mr. McCabe believes has one rather particular defect; it is perpetually tending to destroy that democracy or power of the ordinary man in which Mr. McCabe also believes. Science means specialism, and specialism means oligarchy. If you once establish the habit of trusting particular men to produce particular results in physics or astronomy, you leave the door open for the equally natural demand that you should trust particular men to do particular things in government and the coercing of men. If, you feel it to be reasonable that one beetle should be the only study of one man, and that one man the only student of that one beetle, it is surely a very harmless consequence to go on to say that politics should be the only study of one man, and that one man the only student of politics. As I have pointed out elsewhere in this book, the expert is more aristocratic than the aristocrat, because the aristocrat is only the man who lives well, while the expert is the man who knows better. But if we look at the progress of our scientific civilization we see a gradual increase everywhere of the specialist over the popular function. Once men sang together round a table in chorus; now one man sings alone, for the absurd reason that he can sing better. If scientific civilization goes on (which is most improbable) only one man will laugh, because he can laugh better than the rest.

I do not know that I can express this more shortly than by taking as a text the single sentence of Mr. McCabe, which runs as follows: "The ballets of the Alhambra and the fireworks of the Crystal Palace and Mr. Chesterton's Daily News articles have their places in life." I wish that my articles had as noble a place as either of the other two things mentioned. But let us ask ourselves (in a spirit of love, as Mr. Chadband would say), what are the ballets of the Alhambra? The ballets of the Alhambra are institutions in which a particular selected row of persons in pink go through an operation known as dancing. Now, in all commonwealths dominated by a religion—in the Christian commonwealths of the Middle Ages and in many rude societies—this habit of dancing was a common habit with everybody, and was not necessarily confined to a professional class. A person could dance without being a dancer; a person could dance without being a specialist; a person could dance without being pink. And, in proportion as Mr. McCabe's scientific civilization advances—that is, in proportion as religious civilization (or real civilization) decays—the more and more "well trained," the more and more pink, become the people who do dance, and the more and more numerous become the people who don't. Mr. McCabe may recognize an example of what I mean in the gradual discrediting in society of the ancient European waltz or dance with partners, and the substitution of that horrible and degrading oriental interlude which is known as skirt-dancing. That is the whole essence of decadence, the effacement of five people who do a thing for fun by one person who does it for money. Now it follows, therefore, that when Mr. McCabe says that the ballets of the Alhambra and my articles "have their place in life," it ought to be pointed out to him that he is doing his best to create a world in which dancing, properly speaking, will have no place in life at all. He is, indeed, trying to create a world in which there will be no life for dancing to have a place in. The very fact that Mr. McCabe thinks of dancing as a thing belonging to some hired women at the Alhambra is an illustration of the same principle by which he is able to think of religion as a thing belonging to some hired men in white neckties. Both these things are things which should not be done for us, but by us. If Mr. McCabe were really religious he would be happy. If he were really happy he would dance.

Briefly, we may put the matter in this way. The main point of modern life is not that the Alhambra ballet has its place in life. The main point, the main enormous tragedy of modern life, is that Mr. McCabe has not his place in the Alhambra ballet. The joy of changing and graceful posture, the joy of suiting the swing of music to the swing of limbs, the joy of whirling drapery, the joy of standing on one leg,—all these should belong by rights to Mr. McCabe and to me; in short, to the ordinary healthy citizen. Probably we should not consent to go through these evolutions. But that is because we are miserable moderns and rationalists. We do not merely love ourselves more than we love duty; we actually love ourselves more than we love joy.

When, therefore, Mr. McCabe says that he gives the Alhambra dances (and my articles) their place in life, I think we are justified in pointing out that by the very nature of the case of his philosophy and of his favourite civilization he gives them a very inadequate place. For (if I may pursue the too flattering parallel) Mr. McCabe thinks of the Alhambra and of my articles as two very odd and absurd things, which some special people do (probably for money) in order to amuse him. But if he had ever felt himself the ancient, sublime, elemental, human instinct to dance, he would have discovered that dancing is not a frivolous thing at all, but a very serious thing. He would have discovered that it is the one grave and chaste and decent method of expressing a certain class of emotions. And similarly, if he had ever had, as Mr. Shaw and I have had, the impulse to what he calls paradox, he would have discovered that paradox again is not a frivolous thing, but a very serious thing. He would have found that paradox simply means a certain defiant joy which belongs to belief. I should regard any civilization which was without a universal habit of uproarious dancing as being, from the full human point of view, a defective civilization. And I should regard any mind which had not got the habit in one form or another of uproarious thinking as being, from the full human point of view, a defective mind. It is vain for Mr. McCabe to say that a ballet is a part of him. He should be part of a ballet, or else he is only part of a man. It is in vain for him to say that he is "not quarrelling with the importation of humour into the controversy." He ought himself to be importing humour into every controversy; for unless a man is in part a humorist, he is only in part a man. To sum up the whole matter very simply, if Mr. McCabe asks me why I import frivolity into a discussion of the nature of man, I answer, because frivolity is a part of the nature of man. If he asks me why I introduce what he calls paradoxes into a philosophical problem, I answer, because all philosophical problems tend to become paradoxical. If he objects to my treating of life riotously, I reply that life is a riot. And I say that the Universe as I see it, at any rate, is very much more like the fireworks at the Crystal Palace than it is like his own philosophy. About the whole cosmos there is a tense and secret festivity—like preparations for Guy Fawkes' day. Eternity is the eve of something. I never look up at the stars without feeling that they are the fires of a schoolboy's rocket, fixed in their everlasting fall.

XVII On the Wit of Whistler

That capable and ingenious writer, Mr. Arthur Symons, has included in a book of essays recently published, I believe, an apologia for "London Nights," in which he says that morality should be wholly subordinated to art in criticism, and he uses the somewhat singular argument that art or the worship of beauty is the same in all ages, while morality differs in every period and in every respect. He appears to defy his critics or his readers to mention any permanent feature or quality in ethics. This is surely a very curious example of that extravagant bias against morality which makes so many ultra-modern aesthetes as morbid and fanatical as any Eastern hermit. Unquestionably it is a very common phrase of modern intellectualism to say that the morality of one age can be entirely different to the morality of another. And like a great many other phrases of modern intellectualism, it means literally nothing at all. If the two moralities are entirely different, why do you call them both moralities? It is as if a man said, "Camels in various places are totally diverse; some have six legs, some have none, some have scales, some have feathers, some have horns, some have wings, some are green, some are triangular. There is no point which they have in common." The ordinary man of sense would reply, "Then what makes you call them all camels? What do you mean by a camel? How do you know a camel when you see one?" Of course, there is a permanent substance of morality, as much as there is a permanent substance of art; to say that is only to say that morality is morality, and that art is art. An ideal art critic would, no doubt, see the enduring beauty under every school; equally an ideal moralist would see the enduring ethic under every code. But practically some of the best Englishmen that ever lived could see nothing but filth and idolatry in the starry piety of the Brahmin. And it is equally true that practically the greatest group of artists that the world has ever seen, the giants of the Renaissance, could see nothing but barbarism in the ethereal energy of Gothic.

This bias against morality among the modern aesthetes is nothing very much paraded. And yet it is not really a bias against morality; it is a bias against other people's morality. It is generally founded on a very definite moral preference for a certain sort of life, pagan, plausible, humane. The modern aesthete, wishing us to believe that he values beauty more than conduct, reads Mallarme, and drinks absinthe in a tavern. But this is not only his favourite kind of beauty; it is also his favourite kind of conduct. If he really wished us to believe that he cared for beauty only, he ought to go to nothing but Wesleyan school treats, and paint the sunlight in the hair of the Wesleyan babies. He ought to read nothing but very eloquent theological sermons by old-fashioned Presbyterian divines. Here the lack of all possible moral sympathy would prove that his interest was purely verbal or pictorial, as it is; in all the books he reads and writes he clings to the skirts of his own morality and his own immorality. The champion of l'art pour l'art is always denouncing Ruskin for his moralizing. If he were really a champion of l'art pour l'art, he would be always insisting on Ruskin for his style.

The doctrine of the distinction between art and morality owes a great part of its success to art and morality being hopelessly mixed up in the persons and performances of its greatest exponents. Of this lucky contradiction the very incarnation was Whistler. No man ever preached the impersonality of art so well; no man ever preached the impersonality of art so personally. For him pictures had nothing to do with the problems of character; but for all his fiercest admirers his character was, as a matter of fact far more interesting than his pictures. He gloried in standing as an artist apart from right and wrong. But he succeeded by talking from morning till night about his rights and about his wrongs. His talents were many, his virtues, it must be confessed, not many, beyond that kindness to tried friends, on which many of his biographers insist, but which surely is a quality of all sane men, of pirates and pickpockets; beyond this, his outstanding virtues limit themselves chiefly to two admirable ones—courage and an abstract love of good work. Yet I fancy he won at last more by those two virtues than by all his talents. A man must be something of a moralist if he is to preach, even if he is to preach unmorality. Professor Walter Raleigh, in his "In Memoriam: James McNeill Whistler," insists, truly enough, on the strong streak of an eccentric honesty in matters strictly pictorial, which ran through his complex and slightly confused character. "He would destroy any of his works rather than leave a careless or inexpressive touch within the limits of the frame. He would begin again a hundred times over rather than attempt by patching to make his work seem better than it was."

No one will blame Professor Raleigh, who had to read a sort of funeral oration over Whistler at the opening of the Memorial Exhibition, if, finding himself in that position, he confined himself mostly to the merits and the stronger qualities of his subject. We should naturally go to some other type of composition for a proper consideration of the weaknesses of Whistler. But these must never be omitted from our view of him. Indeed, the truth is that it was not so much a question of the weaknesses of Whistler as of the intrinsic and primary weakness of Whistler. He was one of those people who live up to their emotional incomes, who are always taut and tingling with vanity. Hence he had no strength to spare; hence he had no kindness, no geniality; for geniality is almost definable as strength to spare. He had no god-like carelessness; he never forgot himself; his whole life was, to use his own expression, an arrangement. He went in for "the art of living"—a miserable trick. In a word, he was a great artist; but emphatically not a great man. In this connection I must differ strongly with Professor Raleigh upon what is, from a superficial literary point of view, one of his most effective points. He compares Whistler's laughter to the laughter of another man who was a great man as well as a great artist. "His attitude to the public was exactly the attitude taken up by Robert Browning, who suffered as long a period of neglect and mistake, in those lines of 'The Ring and the Book'—

> "'Well, British Public, ye who like me not,
> (God love you!) and will have your proper laugh
> At the dark question; laugh it! I'd laugh first.'

"Mr. Whistler," adds Professor Raleigh, "always laughed first." The truth is, I believe, that Whistler never laughed at all. There was no laughter in his nature; because there was no thoughtlessness and self-abandonment, no humility. I cannot understand anybody reading "The Gentle Art of Making Enemies" and thinking that there is any laughter in the wit. His wit is a torture to him. He twists himself into arabesques of verbal felicity; he is full of a fierce carefulness; he is inspired with the complete seriousness of sincere malice. He hurts himself to hurt his opponent. Browning did laugh, because Browning did not care; Browning did not care, because Browning was a great man. And when Browning said in brackets to the simple, sensible people who did not like his books, "God love you!" he was not sneering in the least. He was laughing—that is to say, he meant exactly what he said.

There are three distinct classes of great satirists who are also great men—that is to say, three classes of men who can laugh at something without losing their souls. The satirist of the first type is the man who, first of all enjoys himself, and then enjoys his enemies. In this sense he loves his enemy, and by a kind of exaggeration of Christianity he loves his enemy the more the more he becomes an enemy. He has a sort of overwhelming and aggressive happiness in his assertion of anger; his curse is as human as a benediction. Of this type of satire the great example is Rabelais. This is the first typical example of satire, the satire which is voluble, which is violent, which is indecent, but which is not malicious. The satire of Whistler was not this. He was never in any of his controversies simply happy; the proof of it is that he never talked absolute nonsense. There is a second type of mind which produces satire with the quality of greatness. That is embodied in the satirist whose passions are released and let go by some intolerable sense of wrong. He is maddened by the sense of men being maddened; his tongue becomes an unruly member, and testifies against all mankind. Such a man was Swift, in whom the saeva indignatio was a bitterness to others, because it was a bitterness to himself. Such a satirist Whistler was not. He did not laugh because he was happy, like Rabelais. But neither did he laugh because he was unhappy, like Swift.

The third type of great satire is that in which he satirist is enabled to rise superior to his victim in the only serious sense which superiority can bear, in that of pitying the sinner and respecting the man even while he satirises both. Such an achievement can be found in a thing like Pope's "Atticus" a poem in which the satirist feels that he is satirising the weaknesses which belong specially to literary genius. Consequently he takes a pleasure in pointing out his enemy's strength before he points out his weakness. That is, perhaps, the highest and most honourable form of satire. That is not the satire of Whistler. He is not full of a great sorrow for the wrong done to human nature; for him the wrong is altogether done to himself.

He was not a great personality, because he thought so much about himself. And the case is stronger even than that. He was sometimes not even a great artist, because he thought so much about art. Any man with a vital knowledge of the human psychology ought to have the most profound suspicion of anybody who claims to be an artist, and talks a great deal about art. Art is a right and human thing, like walking or saying one's prayers; but the moment it begins to be talked about very solemnly, a man may be fairly certain that the thing has come into a congestion and a kind of difficulty.

The artistic temperament is a disease that afflicts amateurs. It is a disease which arises from men not having sufficient power of expression to utter and get rid of the element of art in their being. It is healthful to every sane man to utter the art within him; it is essential to every sane man to get rid of the art within him at all costs. Artists of a large and wholesome vitality get rid of their art easily, as they breathe easily, or perspire easily. But in artists of less force, the thing becomes a pressure, and produces a definite pain, which is called the artistic temperament. Thus, very great artists are able to be ordinary men—men like Shakespeare or Browning. There are many real tragedies of the artistic temperament, tragedies of vanity or violence or fear. But the great tragedy of the artistic temperament is that it cannot produce any art.

Whistler could produce art; and in so far he was a great man. But he could not forget art; and in so far he was only a man with the artistic temperament. There can be no stronger manifestation of the man who is a really great artist than the fact that he can dismiss the subject of art; that he can, upon due occasion, wish art at the bottom of the sea. Similarly, we should always be much more inclined to trust a solicitor who did not talk about conveyancing over the nuts and wine. What we really desire of any man conducting any business is that the full force of an ordinary man should be put into that particular study. We do not desire that the full force of that study should be put into an ordinary man. We do not in the least wish that our particular law-suit should pour its energy into our barrister's games with his children, or rides on his bicycle, or meditations on the morning star. But we do, as a matter of fact, desire that his games with his children, and his rides on his bicycle, and his meditations on the morning star should pour something of their energy into our law-suit. We do desire that if he has gained any especial lung development from the bicycle, or any bright and pleasing metaphors from the morning star, that the should be placed at our disposal in that particular forensic controversy. In a word, we are very glad that he is an ordinary man, since that may help him to be an exceptional lawyer.

Whistler never ceased to be an artist. As Mr. Max Beerbohm pointed out in one of his extraordinarily sensible and sincere critiques, Whistler really regarded Whistler as his greatest work of art. The white lock, the single eyeglass, the remarkable hat—these were much dearer to him than any nocturnes or arrangements that he ever threw off. He could throw off the nocturnes; for some mysterious reason he could not throw off the hat. He never threw off from himself that disproportionate accumulation of aestheticism which is the burden of the amateur.

It need hardly be said that this is the real explanation of the thing which has puzzled so many dilettante critics, the problem of the extreme ordinariness of the behaviour of so many great geniuses in history. Their behaviour was so ordinary that it was not recorded; hence it was so ordinary that it seemed mysterious. Hence people say that Bacon wrote Shakespeare. The modern artistic temperament cannot understand how a man who could write such lyrics as Shakespeare wrote, could be as keen as Shakespeare was on business transactions in a little town in Warwickshire. The explanation is simple enough; it is that Shakespeare had a real lyrical impulse, wrote a real lyric, and so got rid of the impulse and went about his business. Being an artist did not prevent him from being an ordinary man, any more than being a sleeper at night or being a diner at dinner prevented him from being an ordinary man.

All very great teachers and leaders have had this habit of assuming their point of view to be one which was human and casual, one which would readily appeal to every passing man. If a man is genuinely superior to his fellows the first thing that he believes in is the equality of man. We can see this, for instance, in that strange and innocent rationality with which Christ addressed any motley crowd that happened to stand about Him. "What man of you having a hundred sheep, and losing one, would not leave the ninety and nine in the wilderness, and go after that which was lost?" Or, again, "What man of you if his son ask for bread will he give him a stone, or if he ask for a fish will he give him a serpent?" This plainness, this almost prosaic camaraderie, is the note of all very great minds.

To very great minds the things on which men agree are so immeasurably more important than the things on which they differ, that the latter, for all practical purposes, disappear. They have too much in them of an ancient laughter even to endure to discuss the difference between the hats of two men who were both born of a woman, or between the subtly varied cultures of two men who have both to die. The first-rate great man is equal with other men, like Shakespeare. The second-rate great man is on his knees to other men, like Whitman. The third-rate great man is superior to other men, like Whistler.

XVIII The Fallacy of the Young Nation

To say that a man is an idealist is merely to say that he is a man; but, nevertheless, it might be possible to effect some valid distinction between one kind of idealist and another. One possible distinction, for instance, could be effected by saying that humanity is divided into conscious idealists and unconscious idealists. In a similar way, humanity is divided into conscious ritualists and unconscious ritualists. The curious thing is, in that example as in others, that it is the conscious ritualism which is comparatively simple, the unconscious ritual which is really heavy and complicated. The ritual which is comparatively rude and straightforward is the ritual which people call "ritualistic." It consists of plain things like bread and wine and fire, and men falling on their faces. But the ritual which is really complex, and many coloured, and elaborate, and needlessly formal, is the ritual which people enact without knowing it. It consists not of plain things like wine and fire, but of really peculiar, and local, and exceptional, and ingenious things—things like door-mats, and door-knockers, and electric bells, and silk hats, and white ties, and shiny cards, and confetti. The truth is that the modern man scarcely ever gets back to very old and simple things except when he is performing some religious mummery. The modern man can hardly get away from ritual except by entering a ritualistic church. In the case of these old and mystical formalities we can at least say that the ritual is not mere ritual; that the symbols employed are in most cases symbols which belong to a primary human poetry. The most ferocious opponent of the Christian ceremonials must admit that if Catholicism had not instituted the bread and wine, somebody else would most probably have done so. Any one with a poetical instinct will admit that to the ordinary human instinct bread symbolizes something which cannot very easily be symbolized otherwise; that wine, to the ordinary human instinct, symbolizes something which cannot very easily be symbolized otherwise. But white ties in the evening are ritual, and nothing else but ritual. No one would pretend that white ties in the evening are primary and poetical. Nobody would maintain that the ordinary human instinct would in any age or country tend to symbolize the idea of evening by a white necktie. Rather, the ordinary human instinct would, I imagine, tend to symbolize evening by cravats with some of the colours of the sunset, not white neckties, but tawny or crimson neckties—neckties of purple or olive, or some darkened gold. Mr. J. A. Kensit, for example, is under the impression that he is not a ritualist. But the daily life of Mr. J. A. Kensit, like that of any ordinary modern man, is, as a matter of fact, one continual and compressed catalogue of mystical mummery and flummery. To take one instance out of an inevitable hundred: I imagine that Mr. Kensit takes off his hat to a lady; and what can be more solemn and absurd, considered in the abstract, than, symbolizing the existence of the other sex by taking off a portion of your clothing and waving it in the air? This, I repeat, is not a natural and primitive symbol, like fire or food. A man might just as well have to take off his waistcoat to a lady; and if a man, by the social ritual of his civilization, had to take off his waistcoat to a lady, every chivalrous and sensible man would take off his waistcoat to a lady. In short, Mr. Kensit, and those who agree with him, may think, and quite sincerely think, that men give too much incense and ceremonial to their adoration of the other world. But nobody thinks that he can give too much incense and ceremonial to the adoration of this world. All men, then, are ritualists, but are either conscious or unconscious ritualists. The conscious ritualists are generally satisfied with a few very simple and elementary signs; the unconscious ritualists are not satisfied with anything short of the whole of human life, being almost insanely ritualistic. The first is called a ritualist because he invents and remembers one rite; the other is called an anti-ritualist because he obeys and forgets a thousand. And a somewhat similar distinction to this which I have drawn with some unavoidable length, between the conscious ritualist and the unconscious ritualist, exists between the conscious idealist and the unconscious idealist. It is idle to inveigh against cynics and materialists—there are no cynics, there are no materialists. Every man is idealistic; only it so often happens that he has the wrong ideal. Every man is incurably sentimental; but, unfortunately, it is so often a false sentiment. When we talk, for instance, of some unscrupulous commercial figure, and say that he would do anything for money, we use quite an inaccurate expression, and we slander him very much. He would not do anything for money. He would do some things for money; he would sell his soul for money, for instance; and, as Mirabeau humorously said, he would be quite wise "to take money for muck." He would oppress humanity for money; but then it happens that humanity and the soul are not things that he believes in; they are not his ideals. But he has his own dim and delicate ideals; and he would not violate these for money. He would not drink out of the soup-tureen, for money. He would not wear his coat-tails in front, for money. He would not spread a report that he had softening of the brain, for money. In the actual practice of life we find, in the matter of ideals, exactly what we have already found in the matter of ritual. We find that while there is a perfectly genuine danger of fanaticism from the men who have unworldly ideals, the permanent and urgent danger of fanaticism is from the men who have worldly ideals.

People who say that an ideal is a dangerous thing, that it deludes and intoxicates, are perfectly right. But the ideal which intoxicates most is the least idealistic kind of ideal. The ideal which intoxicates least is the very ideal ideal; that sobers us suddenly, as all heights and precipices and great distances do. Granted that it is a great evil to mistake a cloud for a cape; still, the cloud, which can be most easily mistaken for a cape, is the cloud that is nearest the earth. Similarly, we may grant that it may be dangerous to mistake an ideal for something practical. But we shall still point out that, in this respect, the most dangerous ideal of all is the ideal which looks a little practical. It is difficult to attain a high ideal; consequently, it is almost impossible to persuade ourselves that we have attained it. But it is easy to attain a low ideal; consequently, it is easier still to persuade ourselves that we have attained it when we have done nothing of the kind. To take a random example. It might be called a high ambition to wish to be an archangel; the man who entertained such an ideal would very possibly exhibit asceticism, or even frenzy, but not, I think, delusion. He would not think he was an archangel, and go about flapping his hands under the impression that they were wings. But suppose that a sane man had a low ideal; suppose he wished to be a gentleman. Any one who knows the world knows that in nine weeks he would have persuaded himself that he was a gentleman; and this being manifestly not the case, the result will be very real and practical dislocations and calamities in social life. It is not the wild ideals which wreck the practical world; it is the tame ideals.

The matter may, perhaps, be illustrated by a parallel from our modern politics. When men tell us that the old Liberal politicians of the type of Gladstone cared only for ideals, of course, they are talking nonsense—they cared for a great many other things, including votes. And when men tell us that modern politicians of the type of Mr. Chamberlain or, in another way, Lord Rosebery, care only for votes or for material interest, then again they are talking nonsense—these men care for ideals like all other men. But the real distinction which may be drawn is this, that to the older politician the ideal was an ideal, and nothing else. To the new politician his dream is not only a good dream, it is a reality. The old politician would have said, "It would be a good thing if there were a Republican Federation dominating the world." But the modern politician does not say, "It would be a good thing if there were a British Imperialism dominating the world." He says, "It is a good thing that there is a British Imperialism dominating the world;" whereas clearly there is nothing of the kind. The old Liberal would say "There ought to be a good Irish government in

Ireland." But the ordinary modern Unionist does not say, "There ought to be a good English government in Ireland." He says, "There is a good English government in Ireland;" which is absurd. In short, the modern politicians seem to think that a man becomes practical merely by making assertions entirely about practical things. Apparently, a delusion does not matter as long as it is a materialistic delusion. Instinctively most of us feel that, as a practical matter, even the contrary is true. I certainly would much rather share my apartments with a gentleman who thought he was God than with a gentleman who thought he was a grasshopper. To be continually haunted by practical images and practical problems, to be constantly thinking of things as actual, as urgent, as in process of completion—these things do not prove a man to be practical; these things, indeed, are among the most ordinary signs of a lunatic. That our modern statesmen are materialistic is nothing against their being also morbid. Seeing angels in a vision may make a man a supernaturalist to excess. But merely seeing snakes in delirium tremens does not make him a naturalist.

And when we come actually to examine the main stock notions of our modern practical politicians, we find that those main stock notions are mainly delusions. A great many instances might be given of the fact. We might take, for example, the case of that strange class of notions which underlie the word "union," and all the eulogies heaped upon it. Of course, union is no more a good thing in itself than separation is a good thing in itself. To have a party in favour of union and a party in favour of separation is as absurd as to have a party in favour of going upstairs and a party in favour of going downstairs. The question is not whether we go up or down stairs, but where we are going to, and what we are going, for? Union is strength; union is also weakness. It is a good thing to harness two horses to a cart; but it is not a good thing to try and turn two hansom cabs into one four-wheeler. Turning ten nations into one empire may happen to be as feasible as turning ten shillings into one half-sovereign. Also it may happen to be as preposterous as turning ten terriers into one mastiff. The question in all cases is not a question of union or absence of union, but of identity or absence of identity. Owing to certain historical and moral causes, two nations may be so united as upon the whole to help each other. Thus England and Scotland pass their time in paying each other compliments; but their energies and atmospheres run distinct and parallel, and consequently do not clash. Scotland continues to be educated and Calvinistic; England continues to be uneducated and happy. But owing to certain other Moral and certain other political causes, two nations may be so united as only to hamper each other; their lines do clash and do not run parallel. Thus, for instance, England and Ireland are so united that the Irish can sometimes rule England, but can never rule Ireland. The educational systems, including the last Education Act, are here, as in the case of Scotland, a very good test of the matter. The overwhelming majority of Irishmen believe in a strict Catholicism; the overwhelming majority of Englishmen believe in a vague Protestantism. The Irish party in the Parliament of Union is just large enough to prevent the English education being indefinitely Protestant, and just small enough to prevent the Irish education being definitely Catholic. Here we have a state of things which no man in his senses would ever dream of wishing to continue if he had not been bewitched by the sentimentalism of the mere word "union."

This example of union, however, is not the example which I propose to take of the ingrained futility and deception underlying all the assumptions of the modern practical politician. I wish to speak especially of another and much more general delusion. It pervades the minds and speeches of all the practical men of all parties; and it is a childish blunder built upon a single false metaphor. I refer to the universal modern talk about young nations and new nations; about America being young, about New Zealand being new. The whole thing is a trick of words. America is not young, New Zealand is not new. It is a very discussable question whether they are not both much older than England or Ireland.

Of course we may use the metaphor of youth about America or the colonies, if we use it strictly as implying only a recent origin. But if we use it (as we do use it) as implying vigour, or vivacity, or crudity, or inexperience, or hope, or a long life before them or any of the romantic attributes of youth, then it is surely as clear as daylight that we are duped by a stale figure of speech. We can easily see the matter clearly by applying it to any other institution parallel to the institution of an independent nationality. If a club called "The Milk and Soda League" (let us say) was set up yesterday, as I have no doubt it was, then, of course, "The Milk and Soda League" is a young club in the sense that it was set up yesterday, but in no other sense. It may consist entirely of moribund old gentlemen. It may be moribund itself. We may call it a young club, in the light of the fact that it was founded yesterday. We may also call it a very old club in the light of the fact that it will most probably go bankrupt to-morrow. All this appears very obvious when we put it in this form. Any one who adopted the young-community delusion with regard to a bank or a butcher's shop would be sent to an asylum. But the whole modern political notion that America and the colonies must be very vigorous because they are very new, rests upon no better foundation. That America was founded long after England does not make it even in the faintest degree more probable that America will not perish a long time before England. That England existed before her colonies does not make it any the less likely that she will exist after her colonies. And when we look at the actual history of the world, we find that great European nations almost invariably have survived the vitality of their colonies. When we look at the actual history of the world, we find, that if there is a thing that is born old and dies young, it is a colony. The Greek colonies went to pieces long before the Greek civilization. The Spanish colonies have gone to pieces long before the nation of Spain—nor does there seem to be any reason to doubt the possibility or even the probability of the conclusion that the colonial civilization, which owes its origin to England, will be much briefer and much less vigorous than the civilization of England itself. The English nation will still be going the way of all European nations when the Anglo-Saxon race has gone the way of all fads. Now, of course, the interesting question is, have we, in the case of America and the colonies, any real evidence of a moral and intellectual youth as opposed to the indisputable triviality of a merely chronological youth? Consciously or unconsciously, we know that we have no such evidence, and consciously or unconsciously, therefore, we proceed to make it up. Of this pure and placid invention, a good example, for instance, can be found in a recent poem of Mr. Rudyard Kipling's. Speaking of the English people and the South African War Mr. Kipling says that "we fawned on the younger nations for the men that could shoot and ride." Some people considered this sentence insulting. All that I am concerned with at present is the evident fact that it is not true. The colonies provided very useful volunteer troops, but they did not provide the best troops, nor achieve the most successful exploits. The best work in the war on the English side was done, as might have been expected, by the best English regiments. The men who could shoot and ride were not the enthusiastic corn merchants from Melbourne, any more than they were the enthusiastic clerks from Cheapside. The men who could shoot and ride were the men who had been taught to shoot and ride in the discipline of the standing army of a great European power. Of course, the colonials are as brave and athletic as any other average white men. Of course, they acquitted themselves with reasonable credit. All I have here to indicate is that, for the purposes of this theory of the new nation, it is necessary to maintain that the colonial forces were more useful or more heroic than the gunners at Colenso or the Fighting Fifth. And of this contention there is not, and never has been, one stick or straw of evidence.

A similar attempt is made, and with even less success, to represent the literature of the colonies as something fresh and vigorous and important. The imperialist magazines are constantly springing upon us some genius from Queensland or Canada, through whom we are expected to smell the odours of the bush or the prairie. As a matter of fact, any one who is even slightly interested in literature as such (and I, for one, confess that I am only slightly interested in literature as such), will freely admit that the stories of these geniuses smell of nothing but printer's ink, and that not of first-rate quality. By a great effort of Imperial imagination the generous English people reads into these works a force and a novelty. But the force and the novelty are not in the new writers; the force and the novelty are in the ancient heart of the English. Anybody who studies them impartially will know that the first-rate writers of the colonies are not even particularly novel in their note and atmosphere, are not only not producing a new kind of good literature, but are not even in any particular sense producing a new kind of bad literature. The first-rate writers of the new countries are really almost exactly like the second-rate writers of the old countries. Of course they do feel the mystery of the wilderness, the mystery of the bush, for all simple and honest men feel this in Melbourne, or Margate, or South St. Pancras. But when they write most sincerely and most successfully, it is not with a background of the mystery of the bush, but with a background, expressed or assumed, of our own romantic cockney civilization. What really moves their souls with a kindly terror is not the mystery of the wilderness, but the Mystery of a Hansom Cab.

Of course there are some exceptions to this generalization. The one really arresting exception is Olive Schreiner, and she is quite as certainly an exception that proves the rule. Olive Schreiner is a fierce, brilliant, and realistic novelist; but she is all this precisely because she is not English at all. Her tribal kinship is with the country of Teniers and Maarten Maartens—that is, with a country of realists. Her literary kinship is with the pessimistic fiction of the continent; with the novelists whose very pity is cruel. Olive Schreiner is the one English colonial who is not conventional, for the simple reason that South Africa is the one English colony which is not English, and probably never will be. And, of course, there are individual exceptions in a minor way. I remember in particular some Australian tales by Mr. McIlwain which were really able and effective, and which, for that reason, I suppose, are not presented to the public with blasts of a trumpet. But my general contention if put before any one with a love of letters, will not be disputed if it is understood. It is not the truth that the colonial civilization as a whole is giving us, or shows any signs of giving us, a literature which will startle and renovate our own. It may be a very good thing for us to have an affectionate illusion in the matter; that is quite another affair. The colonies may have given England a new emotion; I only say that they have not given the world a new book.

Touching these English colonies, I do not wish to be misunderstood. I do not say of them or of America that they have not a future, or that they will not be great nations. I merely deny the whole established modern expression about them. I deny that they are "destined" to a future. I deny that they are "destined" to be great nations. I deny (of course) that any human thing is destined to be anything. All the absurd physical metaphors, such as youth and age, living and dying, are, when applied to nations, but pseudo-scientific attempts to conceal from men the awful liberty of their lonely souls.

In the case of America, indeed, a warning to this effect is instant and essential. America, of course, like every other human thing, can in spiritual sense live or die as much as it chooses. But at the present moment the matter which America has very seriously to consider is not how near it is to its birth and beginning, but how near it may be to its end. It is only a verbal question whether the American civilization is young; it may become a very practical and urgent question whether it is dying. When once we have cast aside, as we inevitably have after a moment's thought, the fanciful physical metaphor involved in the word "youth," what serious evidence have we that America is a fresh force and not a stale one? It has a great many people, like China; it has a great deal of money, like defeated Carthage or dying Venice. It is full of bustle and excitability, like Athens after its ruin, and all the Greek cities in their decline. It is fond of new things; but the old are always fond of new things. Young men read chronicles, but old men read newspapers. It admires strength and good looks; it admires a big and barbaric beauty in its women, for instance; but so did Rome when the Goth was at the gates. All these are things quite compatible with fundamental tedium and decay. There are three main shapes or symbols in which a nation can show itself essentially glad and great—by the heroic in government, by the heroic in arms, and by the heroic in art. Beyond government, which is, as it were, the very shape and body of a nation, the most significant thing about any citizen is his artistic attitude towards a holiday and his moral attitude towards a fight—that is, his way of accepting life and his way of accepting death.

Subjected to these eternal tests, America does not appear by any means as particularly fresh or untouched. She appears with all the weakness and weariness of modern England or of any other Western power. In her politics she has broken up exactly as England has broken up, into a bewildering opportunism and insincerity. In the matter of war and the national attitude towards war, her resemblance to England is even more manifest and melancholy. It may be said with rough accuracy that there are three stages in the life of a strong people. First, it is a small power, and fights small powers. Then it is a great power, and fights great powers. Then it is a great power, and fights small powers, but pretends that they are great powers, in order to rekindle the ashes of its ancient emotion and vanity. After that, the next step is to become a small power itself. England exhibited this symptom of decadence very badly in the war with the Transvaal; but America exhibited it worse in the war with Spain. There was exhibited more sharply and absurdly than anywhere else the ironic contrast between the very careless choice of a strong line and the very careful choice of a weak enemy. America added to all her other late Roman or Byzantine elements the element of the Caracallan triumph, the triumph over nobody.

But when we come to the last test of nationality, the test of art and letters, the case is almost terrible. The English colonies have produced no great artists; and that fact may prove that they are still full of silent possibilities and reserve force. But America has produced great artists. And that fact most certainly proves that she is full of a fine futility and the end of all things. Whatever the American men of genius are, they are not young gods making a young world. Is the art of Whistler a brave, barbaric art, happy and headlong? Does Mr. Henry James infect us with the spirit of a schoolboy? No; the colonies have not spoken, and they are safe. Their silence may be the silence of the unborn. But out of America has come a sweet and startling cry, as unmistakable as the cry of a dying man.

XIX Slum Novelists and the Slums

Odd ideas are entertained in our time about the real nature of the doctrine of human fraternity. The real doctrine is something which we do not, with all our modern humanitarianism, very clearly understand, much less very closely practise. There is nothing, for instance, particularly undemocratic about kicking your butler downstairs. It may be wrong, but it is not unfraternal. In a certain sense, the blow or kick may be considered as a confession of equality: you are meeting your butler body to body; you are almost according him the privilege of the duel. There is nothing, undemocratic, though there may be something unreasonable, in expecting a great deal from the butler, and being filled with a kind of frenzy of surprise when he falls short of the divine stature. The thing which is really undemocratic and unfraternal is not to expect the butler to be more or less divine. The thing which is really undemocratic and unfraternal is to say, as so many modern humanitarians say, "Of course one must make allowances for those on a lower plane." All things considered indeed, it may be said, without undue exaggeration, that the really undemocratic and unfraternal thing is the common practice of not kicking the butler downstairs.

It is only because such a vast section of the modern world is out of sympathy with the serious democratic sentiment that this statement will seem to many to be lacking in seriousness. Democracy is not philanthropy; it is not even altruism or social reform. Democracy is not founded on pity for the common man; democracy is founded on reverence for the common man, or, if you will, even on fear of him. It does not champion man because man is so miserable, but because man is so sublime. It does not object so much to the ordinary man being a slave as to his not being a king, for its dream is always the dream of the first Roman republic, a nation of kings.

Next to a genuine republic, the most democratic thing in the world is a hereditary despotism. I mean a despotism in which there is absolutely no trace whatever of any nonsense about intellect or special fitness for the post. Rational despotism—that is, selective despotism—is always a curse to mankind, because with that you have the ordinary man misunderstood and misgoverned by some prig who has no brotherly respect for him at all. But irrational despotism is always democratic, because it is the ordinary man enthroned. The worst form of slavery is that which is called Caesarism, or the choice of some bold or brilliant man as despot because he is suitable. For that means that men choose a representative, not because he represents them, but because he does not. Men trust an ordinary man like George III or William IV. because they are themselves ordinary men and understand him. Men trust an ordinary man because they trust themselves. But men trust a great man because they do not trust themselves. And hence the worship of great men always appears in times of weakness and cowardice; we never hear of great men until the time when all other men are small.

Hereditary despotism is, then, in essence and sentiment democratic because it chooses from mankind at random. If it does not declare that every man may rule, it declares the next most democratic thing; it declares that any man may rule. Hereditary aristocracy is a far worse and more dangerous thing, because the numbers and multiplicity of an aristocracy make it sometimes possible for it to figure as an aristocracy of intellect. Some of its members will presumably have brains, and thus they, at any rate, will be an intellectual aristocracy within the social one. They will rule the aristocracy by virtue of their intellect, and they will rule the country by virtue of their aristocracy. Thus a double falsity will be set up, and millions of the images of God, who, fortunately for their wives and families, are neither gentlemen nor clever men, will be represented by a man like Mr. Balfour or Mr. Wyndham, because he is too gentlemanly to be called merely clever, and just too clever to be called merely a gentleman. But even an hereditary aristocracy may exhibit, by a sort of accident, from time to time some of the basically democratic quality which belongs to a hereditary despotism. It is amusing to think how much conservative ingenuity has been wasted in the defence of the House of Lords by men who were desperately endeavouring to prove that the House of Lords consisted of clever men. There is one really good defence of the House of Lords, though admirers of the peerage are strangely coy about using it; and that is, that the House of Lords, in its full and proper strength, consists of stupid men. It really would be a plausible defence of that otherwise indefensible body to point out that the clever men in the Commons, who owed their power to cleverness, ought in the last resort to be checked by the average man in the Lords, who owed their power to accident. Of course, there would be many answers to such a contention, as, for instance, that the House of Lords is largely no longer a House of Lords, but a House of tradesmen and financiers, or that the bulk of the commonplace nobility do not vote, and so leave the chamber to the prigs and the specialists and the mad old gentlemen with hobbies. But on some occasions the House of Lords, even under all these disadvantages, is in some sense representative. When all the peers flocked together to vote against Mr. Gladstone's second Home Rule Bill, for instance, those who said that the peers represented the English people, were perfectly right. All those dear old men who happened to be born peers were at that moment, and upon that question, the precise counterpart of all the dear old men who happened to be born paupers or middle-class gentlemen. That mob of peers did really represent the English people—that is to say, it was honest, ignorant, vaguely excited, almost unanimous, and obviously wrong. Of course, rational democracy is better as an expression of the public will than the haphazard hereditary method. While we are about having any kind of democracy, let it be rational democracy. But if we are to have any kind of oligarchy, let it be irrational oligarchy. Then at least we shall be ruled by men.

But the thing which is really required for the proper working of democracy is not merely the democratic system, or even the democratic philosophy, but the democratic emotion. The democratic emotion, like most elementary and indispensable things, is a thing difficult to describe at any time. But it is peculiarly difficult to describe it in our enlightened age, for the simple reason that it is peculiarly difficult to find it. It is a certain instinctive attitude which feels the things in which all men agree to be unspeakably important, and all the things in which they differ (such as mere brains) to be almost unspeakably unimportant. The nearest approach to it in our ordinary life would be the promptitude with which we should consider mere humanity in any circumstance of shock or death. We should say, after a somewhat disturbing discovery, "There is a dead man under the sofa." We should not be likely to say, "There is a dead man of considerable personal refinement under the sofa." We should say, "A woman has fallen into the water." We should not say, "A highly educated woman has fallen into the water." Nobody would say, "There are the remains of a clear thinker in your back garden." Nobody would say, "Unless you hurry up and stop him, a man with a very fine ear for music will have jumped off that cliff." But this emotion, which all of us have in connection with such things as birth and death, is to some people native and constant at all ordinary times and in all ordinary places. It was native to St. Francis of Assisi. It was native to Walt Whitman. In this strange and splendid degree it cannot be expected, perhaps, to pervade a whole commonwealth or a whole civilization; but one commonwealth may have it much more than another commonwealth, one civilization much more than another civilization. No community, perhaps, ever had it so much as the early Franciscans. No community, perhaps, ever had it so little as ours.

Everything in our age has, when carefully examined, this fundamentally undemocratic quality. In religion and morals we should admit, in the abstract, that the sins of the educated classes were as great as, or perhaps greater than, the sins of the poor and ignorant. But in practice the great difference between the mediaeval ethics and ours is that ours concentrate attention on the sins which are the sins of the ignorant, and practically deny that the sins which are the sins of the educated are sins at all. We are always talking about the sin of intemperate drinking, because it is quite obvious that the poor have it more than the rich. But we are always denying that there is any such thing as the sin of pride, because it would be quite obvious that the rich have it more than the poor. We are always ready to make a saint or prophet of the educated man who goes into cottages to give a little kindly advice to the uneducated. But the medieval idea of a saint or prophet was something quite different. The mediaeval saint or prophet was an uneducated man who walked into grand houses to give a little kindly advice to the educated. The old tyrants had enough insolence to despoil the poor, but they had not enough insolence to preach to them. It was the gentleman who oppressed the slums; but it was the slums that admonished the gentleman. And just as we are undemocratic in faith and morals, so we are, by the very nature of our attitude in such matters, undemocratic in the tone of our practical politics. It is a sufficient proof that we are not an essentially democratic state that we are always wondering what we shall do with the poor. If we were democrats, we should be wondering what the poor will do with us. With us the governing class is always saying to itself, "What laws shall we make?" In a purely democratic state it would be always saying, "What laws can we obey?" A purely democratic state perhaps there has never been. But even the feudal ages were in practice thus far democratic, that every feudal potentate knew that any laws which he made would in all probability return upon himself. His feathers might be cut off for breaking a sumptuary law. His head might be cut off for high treason. But the modern laws are almost always laws made to affect the governed class, but not the governing. We have public-house licensing laws, but not sumptuary laws. That is to say, we have laws against the festivity and hospitality of the poor, but no laws against the festivity and hospitality of the rich. We have laws against blasphemy—that is, against a kind of coarse and offensive speaking in which nobody but a rough and obscure man would be likely to indulge. But we have no laws against heresy—that is, against the intellectual poisoning of the whole people, in which only a prosperous and prominent man would be likely to be successful. The evil of aristocracy is not that it necessarily leads to the infliction of bad things or the suffering of sad ones; the evil of aristocracy is that it places everything in the hands of a class of people who can always inflict what they can never suffer. Whether what they inflict is, in their intention, good or bad, they become equally frivolous. The case against the governing class of modern England is not in the least that it is selfish; if you like, you may call the English oligarchs too fantastically unselfish. The case against them simply is that when they legislate for all men, they always omit themselves.

We are undemocratic, then, in our religion, as is proved by our efforts to "raise" the poor. We are undemocratic in our government, as is proved by our innocent attempt to govern them well. But above all we are undemocratic in our literature, as is proved by the torrent of novels about the poor and serious studies of the poor which pour from our publishers every month. And the more "modern" the book is the more certain it is to be devoid of democratic sentiment.

A poor man is a man who has not got much money. This may seem a simple and unnecessary description, but in the face of a great mass of modern fact and fiction, it seems very necessary indeed; most of our realists and sociologists talk about a poor man as if he were an octopus or an alligator. There is no more need to study the psychology of poverty than to study the psychology of bad temper, or the psychology of vanity, or the psychology of animal spirits. A man ought to know something of the emotions of an insulted man, not by being insulted, but simply by being a man. And he ought to know something of the emotions of a poor man, not by being poor, but simply by being a man. Therefore, in any writer who is describing poverty, my first objection to him will be that he has studied his subject. A democrat would have imagined it.

A great many hard things have been said about religious slumming and political or social slumming, but surely the most despicable of all is artistic slumming. The religious teacher is at least supposed to be interested in the costermonger because he is a man; the politician is in some dim and perverted sense interested in the costermonger because he is a citizen; it is only the wretched writer who is interested in the costermonger merely because he is a costermonger. Nevertheless, so long as he is merely seeking impressions, or in other words copy, his trade, though dull, is honest. But when he endeavours to represent that he is describing the spiritual core of a costermonger, his dim vices and his delicate virtues, then we must object that his claim is preposterous; we must remind him that he is a journalist and nothing else. He has far less psychological authority even than the foolish missionary. For he is in the literal and derivative sense a journalist, while the missionary is an eternalist. The missionary at least pretends to have a version of the man's lot for all time; the journalist only pretends to have a version of it from day to day. The missionary comes to tell the poor man that he is in the same condition with all men. The journalist comes to tell other people how different the poor man is from everybody else.

If the modern novels about the slums, such as novels of Mr. Arthur Morrison, or the exceedingly able novels of Mr. Somerset Maugham, are intended to be sensational, I can only say that that is a noble and reasonable object, and that they attain it. A sensation, a shock to the imagination, like the contact with cold water, is always a good and exhilarating thing; and, undoubtedly, men will always seek this sensation (among other forms) in the form of the study of the strange antics of remote or alien peoples.

In the twelfth century men obtained this sensation by reading about dog-headed men in Africa. In the twentieth century they obtained it by reading about pig-headed Boers in Africa. The men of the twentieth century were certainly, it must be admitted, somewhat the more credulous of the two. For it is not recorded of the men in the twelfth century that they organized a sanguinary crusade solely for the purpose of altering the singular formation of the heads of the Africans. But it may be, and it may even legitimately be, that since all these monsters have faded from the popular mythology, it is necessary to have in our fiction the image of the horrible and hairy East-ender, merely to keep alive in us a fearful and childlike wonder at external peculiarities. But the Middle Ages (with a great deal more common sense than it would now be fashionable to admit) regarded natural history at bottom rather as a kind of joke; they regarded the soul as very important. Hence, while they had a natural history of dog-headed men, they did not profess to have a psychology of dog-headed men. They did not profess to mirror the mind of a dog-headed man, to share his tenderest secrets, or mount with his most celestial musings. They did not write novels about the semi-canine creature, attributing to him all the oldest morbidities and all the newest fads. It is permissible to present men as monsters if we wish to make the reader jump; and to make anybody jump is always a Christian act. But it is not permissible to present men as regarding themselves as monsters, or as making themselves jump. To summarize, our slum fiction is quite defensible as aesthetic fiction; it is not defensible as spiritual fact.

One enormous obstacle stands in the way of its actuality. The men who write it, and the men who read it, are men of the middle classes or the upper classes; at least, of those who are loosely termed the educated classes. Hence, the fact that it is the life as the refined man sees it proves that it cannot be the life as the unrefined man lives it. Rich men write stories about poor men, and describe them as speaking with a coarse, or heavy, or husky enunciation. But if poor men wrote novels about you or me they would describe us as speaking with some absurd shrill and affected voice, such as we only hear from a duchess in a three-act farce. The slum novelist gains his whole effect by the fact that some detail is strange to the reader; but that detail by the nature of the case cannot be strange in itself. It cannot be strange to the soul which he is professing to study. The slum novelist gains his effects by describing the same grey mist as draping the dingy factory and the dingy tavern. But to the man he is supposed to be studying there must be exactly the same difference between the factory and the tavern that there is to a middle-class man between a late night at the office and a supper at Pagani's. The slum novelist is content with pointing out that to the eye of his particular class a pickaxe looks dirty and a pewter pot looks dirty. But the man he is supposed to be studying sees the difference between them exactly as a clerk sees the difference between a ledger and an edition de luxe. The chiaroscuro of the life is inevitably lost; for to us the high lights and the shadows are a light grey. But the high lights and the shadows are not a light grey in that life any more than in any other. The kind of man who could really express the pleasures of the poor would be also the kind of man who could share them. In short, these books are not a record of the psychology of poverty. They are a record of the psychology of wealth and culture when brought in contact with poverty. They are not a description of the state of the slums. They are only a very dark and dreadful description of the state of the slummers. One might give innumerable examples of the essentially unsympathetic and unpopular quality of these realistic writers. But perhaps the simplest and most obvious example with which we could conclude is the mere fact that these writers are realistic. The poor have many other vices, but, at least, they are never realistic. The poor are melodramatic and romantic in grain; the poor all believe in high moral platitudes and copy-book maxims; probably this is the ultimate meaning of the great saying, "Blessed are the poor." Blessed are the poor, for they are always making life, or trying to make life like an Adelphi play. Some innocent educationalists and philanthropists (for even philanthropists can be innocent) have expressed a grave astonishment that the masses prefer shilling shockers to scientific treatises and melodramas to problem plays. The reason is very simple. The realistic story is certainly more artistic than the melodramatic story. If what you desire is deft handling, delicate proportions, a unit of artistic atmosphere, the realistic story has a full advantage over the melodrama. In everything that is light and bright and ornamental the realistic story has a full advantage over the melodrama. But, at least, the melodrama has one indisputable advantage over the realistic story. The melodrama is much more like life. It is much more like man, and especially the poor man. It is very banal and very inartistic when a poor woman at the Adelphi says, "Do you think I will sell my own child?" But poor women in the Battersea High Road do say, "Do you think I will sell my own child?" They say it on every available occasion; you can hear a sort of murmur or babble of it all the way down the street. It is very stale and weak dramatic art (if that is all) when the workman confronts his master and says, "I'm a man." But a workman does say "I'm a man" two or three times every day. In fact, it is tedious, possibly, to hear poor men being melodramatic behind the footlights; but that is because one can always hear them being melodramatic in the street outside. In short, melodrama, if it is dull, is dull because it is too accurate. Somewhat the same problem exists in the case of stories about schoolboys. Mr. Kipling's "Stalky and Co." is much more amusing (if you are talking about amusement) than the late Dean Farrar's "Eric; or, Little by Little." But "Eric" is immeasurably more like real school-life. For real school-life, real boyhood, is full of the things of which Eric is full—priggishness, a crude piety, a silly sin, a weak but continual attempt at the heroic, in a word, melodrama. And if we wish to lay a firm basis for any efforts to help the poor, we must not become realistic and see them from the outside. We must become melodramatic, and see them from the inside. The novelist must not take out his notebook and say, "I am an expert." No; he must imitate the workman in the Adelphi play. He must slap himself on the chest and say, "I am a man."

XX. Concluding Remarks on the Importance of Orthodoxy

Whether the human mind can advance or not, is a question too little discussed, for nothing can be more dangerous than to found our social philosophy on any theory which is debatable but has not been debated. But if we assume, for the sake of argument, that there has been in the past, or will be in the future, such a thing as a growth or improvement of the human mind itself, there still remains a very sharp objection to be raised against the modern version of that improvement. The vice of the modern notion of mental progress is that it is always something concerned with the breaking of bonds, the effacing of boundaries, the casting away of dogmas. But if there be such a thing as mental growth, it must mean the growth into more and more definite convictions, into more and more dogmas. The human brain is a machine for coming to conclusions; if it cannot come to conclusions it is rusty. When we hear of a man too clever to believe, we are hearing of something having almost the character of a contradiction in terms. It is like hearing of a nail that was too good to hold down a carpet; or a bolt that was too strong to keep a door shut. Man can hardly be defined, after the fashion of Carlyle, as an animal who makes tools; ants and beavers and many other animals make tools, in the sense that they make an apparatus. Man can be defined as an animal that makes dogmas. As he piles doctrine on doctrine and conclusion on conclusion in the formation of some tremendous scheme of philosophy and religion, he is, in the only legitimate sense of which the expression is capable, becoming more and more human. When he drops one doctrine after another in a refined scepticism, when he declines to tie himself to a system, when he says that he has outgrown definitions, when he says that he disbelieves in finality, when, in his own imagination, he sits as God, holding no form of creed but contemplating all, then he is by that very process sinking slowly backwards into the vagueness of the vagrant animals and the unconsciousness of the grass. Trees have no dogmas. Turnips are singularly broad-minded.

If then, I repeat, there is to be mental advance, it must be mental advance in the construction of a definite philosophy of life. And that philosophy of life must be right and the other philosophies wrong. Now of all, or nearly all, the able modern writers whom I have briefly studied in this book, this is especially and pleasingly true, that they do each of them have a constructive and affirmative view, and that they do take it seriously and ask us to take it seriously. There is nothing merely sceptically progressive about Mr. Rudyard Kipling. There is nothing in the least broad minded about Mr. Bernard Shaw. The paganism of Mr. Lowes Dickinson is more grave than any Christianity. Even the opportunism of Mr. H. G. Wells is more dogmatic than the idealism of anybody else. Somebody complained, I think, to Matthew Arnold that he was getting as dogmatic as Carlyle. He replied, "That may be true; but you overlook an obvious difference. I am dogmatic and right, and Carlyle is dogmatic and wrong." The strong humour of the remark ought not to disguise from us its everlasting seriousness and common sense; no man ought to write at all, or even to speak at all, unless he thinks that he is in truth and the other man in error. In similar style, I hold that I am dogmatic and right, while Mr. Shaw is dogmatic and wrong. But my main point, at present, is to notice that the chief among these writers I have discussed do most sanely and courageously offer themselves as dogmatists, as founders of a system. It may be true that the thing in Mr. Shaw most interesting to me, is the fact that Mr. Shaw is wrong. But it is equally true that the thing in Mr. Shaw most interesting to himself, is the fact that Mr. Shaw is right. Mr. Shaw may have none with him but himself; but it is not for himself he cares. It is for the vast and universal church, of which he is the only member.

The two typical men of genius whom I have mentioned here, and with whose names I have begun this book, are very symbolic, if only because they have shown that the fiercest dogmatists can make the best artists. In the fin de siecle atmosphere every one was crying out that literature should be free from all causes and all ethical creeds. Art was to produce only exquisite workmanship, and it was especially the note of those days to demand brilliant plays and brilliant short stories. And when they got them, they got them from a couple of moralists. The best short stories were written by a man trying to preach Imperialism. The best plays were written by a man trying to preach Socialism. All the art of all the artists looked tiny and tedious beside the art which was a byproduct of propaganda.

The reason, indeed, is very simple. A man cannot be wise enough to be a great artist without being wise enough to wish to be a philosopher. A man cannot have the energy to produce good art without having the energy to wish to pass beyond it. A small artist is content with art; a great artist is content with nothing except everything. So we find that when real forces, good or bad, like Kipling and G. B. S., enter our arena, they bring with them not only startling and arresting art, but very startling and arresting dogmas. And they care even more, and desire us to care even more, about their startling and arresting dogmas than about their startling and arresting art. Mr. Shaw is a good dramatist, but what he desires more than anything else to be is a good politician. Mr. Rudyard Kipling is by divine caprice and natural genius an unconventional poet; but what he desires more than anything else to be is a conventional poet. He desires to be the poet of his people, bone of their bone, and flesh of their flesh, understanding their origins, celebrating their destiny. He desires to be Poet Laureate, a most sensible and honourable and public-spirited desire. Having been given by the gods originality—that is, disagreement with others—he desires divinely to agree with them. But the most striking instance of all, more striking, I think, even than either of these, is the instance of Mr. H. G. Wells. He began in a sort of insane infancy of pure art. He began by making a new heaven and a new earth, with the same irresponsible instinct by which men buy a new necktie or button-hole. He began by trifling with the stars and systems in order to make ephemeral anecdotes; he killed the universe for a joke. He has since become more and more serious, and has become, as men inevitably do when they become more and more serious, more and more parochial. He was frivolous about the twilight of the gods; but he is serious about the London omnibus. He was careless in "The Time Machine," for that dealt only with the destiny of all things; but he is careful, and even cautious, in "Mankind in the Making," for that deals with the day after to-morrow. He began with the end of the world, and that was easy. Now he has gone on to the beginning of the world, and that is difficult. But the main result of all this is the same as in the other cases. The men who have really been the bold artists, the realistic artists, the uncompromising artists, are the men who have turned out, after all, to be writing "with a purpose." Suppose that any cool and cynical art-critic, any art-critic fully impressed with the conviction that artists were greatest when they were most purely artistic, suppose that a man who professed ably a humane aestheticism, as did Mr. Max Beerbohm, or a cruel aestheticism, as did Mr. W. E. Henley, had cast his eye over the whole fictional literature which was recent in the year 1895, and had been asked to select the three most vigorous and promising and original artists and artistic works, he would, I think, most certainly have said that for a fine artistic audacity, for a real artistic delicacy, or for a whiff of true novelty in art, the things that stood first were "Soldiers Three," by a Mr. Rudyard Kipling; "Arms and the Man," by a Mr. Bernard Shaw; and "The Time Machine," by a man called Wells. And all these men have shown themselves ingrainedly didactic. You may express the matter if you will by saying that if we want doctrines we go to the great artists. But it is clear from the psychology of the matter that this is not the true statement; the true statement is that when we want any art tolerably brisk and bold we have to go to the doctrinaires.

In concluding this book, therefore, I would ask, first and foremost, that men such as these of whom I have spoken should not be insulted by being taken for artists. No man has any right whatever merely to enjoy the work of Mr. Bernard Shaw; he might as well enjoy the invasion of his country by the French. Mr. Shaw writes either to convince or to enrage us. No man has any business to be a Kiplingite without being a politician, and an Imperialist politician. If a man is first with us, it should be because of what is first with him. If a man convinces us at all, it should be by his convictions. If we hate a poem of Kipling's from political passion, we are hating it for the same reason that the poet loved it; if we dislike him because of his opinions, we are disliking him for the best of all possible reasons. If a man comes into Hyde Park to preach it is permissible to hoot him; but it is discourteous to applaud him as a performing bear. And an artist is only a performing bear compared with the meanest man who fancies he has anything to say.

There is, indeed, one class of modern writers and thinkers who cannot altogether be overlooked in this question, though there is no space here for a lengthy account of them, which, indeed, to confess the truth, would consist chiefly of abuse. I mean those who get over all these abysses and reconcile all these wars by talking about "aspects of truth," by saying that the art of Kipling represents one aspect of the truth, and the art of William Watson another; the art of Mr. Bernard Shaw one aspect of the truth, and the art of Mr. Cunningham Grahame another; the art of Mr. H. G. Wells one aspect, and the art of Mr. Coventry Patmore (say) another. I will only say here that this seems to me an evasion which has not even had the sense to disguise itself ingeniously in words. If we talk of a certain thing being an aspect of truth, it is evident that we claim to know what is truth; just as, if we talk of the hind leg of a dog, we claim to know what is a dog. Unfortunately, the philosopher who talks about aspects of truth generally also asks, "What is truth?" Frequently even he denies the existence of truth, or says it is inconceivable by the human intelligence. How, then, can he recognize its aspects? I should not like to be an artist who brought an architectural sketch to a builder, saying, "This is the south aspect of Sea-View Cottage. Sea-View Cottage, of course, does not exist." I should not even like very much to have to explain, under such circumstances, that Sea-View Cottage might exist, but was unthinkable by the human mind. Nor should I like any better to be the bungling and absurd metaphysician who professed to be able to see everywhere the aspects of a truth that is not there. Of course, it is perfectly obvious that there are truths in Kipling, that there are truths in Shaw or Wells. But the degree to which we can perceive them depends strictly upon how far we have a definite conception inside us of what is truth. It is ludicrous to suppose that the more sceptical we are the more we see good in everything. It is clear that the more we are certain what good is, the more we shall see good in everything.

I plead, then, that we should agree or disagree with these men. I plead that we should agree with them at least in having an abstract belief. But I know that there are current in the modern world many vague objections to having an abstract belief, and I feel that we shall not get any further until we have dealt with some of them. The first objection is easily stated.

A common hesitation in our day touching the use of extreme convictions is a sort of notion that extreme convictions specially upon cosmic matters, have been responsible in the past for the thing which is called bigotry. But a very small amount of direct experience will dissipate this view. In real life the people who are most bigoted are the people who have no convictions at all. The economists of the Manchester school who disagree with Socialism take Socialism seriously. It is the young man in Bond Street, who does not know what socialism means much less whether he agrees with it, who is quite certain that these socialist fellows are making a fuss about nothing. The man who understands the Calvinist philosophy enough to agree with it must understand the Catholic philosophy in order to disagree with it. It is the vague modern who is not at all certain what is right who is most certain that Dante was wrong. The serious opponent of the Latin Church in history, even in the act of showing that it produced great infamies, must know that it produced great saints. It is the hard-headed stockbroker, who knows no history and believes no religion, who is, nevertheless, perfectly convinced that all these priests are knaves. The Salvationist at the Marble Arch may be bigoted, but he is not too bigoted to yearn from a common human kinship after the dandy on church parade. But the dandy on church parade is so bigoted that he does not in the least yearn after the Salvationist at the Marble Arch. Bigotry may be roughly defined as the anger of men who have no opinions. It is the resistance offered to definite ideas by that vague bulk of people whose ideas are indefinite to excess. Bigotry may be called the appalling frenzy of the indifferent. This frenzy of the indifferent is in truth a terrible thing; it has made all monstrous and widely pervading persecutions. In this degree it was not the people who cared who ever persecuted; the people who cared were not sufficiently numerous. It was the people who did not care who filled the world with fire and oppression. It was the hands of the indifferent that lit the faggots; it was the hands of the indifferent that turned the rack. There have come some persecutions out of the pain of a passionate certainty; but these produced, not bigotry, but fanaticism—a very different and a somewhat admirable thing. Bigotry in the main has always been the pervading omnipotence of those who do not care crushing out those who care in darkness and blood.

There are people, however, who dig somewhat deeper than this into the possible evils of dogma. It is felt by many that strong philosophical conviction, while it does not (as they perceive) produce that sluggish and fundamentally frivolous condition which we call bigotry, does produce a certain concentration, exaggeration, and moral impatience, which we may agree to call fanaticism. They say, in brief, that ideas are dangerous things. In politics, for example, it is commonly urged against a man like Mr. Balfour, or against a man like Mr. John Morley, that a wealth of ideas is dangerous. The true doctrine on this point, again, is surely not very difficult to state. Ideas are dangerous, but the man to whom they are least dangerous is the man of ideas. He is acquainted with ideas, and moves among them like a lion-tamer. Ideas are dangerous, but the man to whom they are most dangerous is the man of no ideas. The man of no ideas will find the first idea fly to his head like wine to the head of a teetotaller. It is a common error, I think, among the Radical idealists of my own party and period to suggest that financiers and business men are a danger to the empire because they are so sordid or so materialistic. The truth is that financiers and business men are a danger to the empire because they can be sentimental about any sentiment, and idealistic about any ideal, any ideal that they find lying about. just as a boy who has not known much of women is apt too easily to take a woman for the woman, so these practical men, unaccustomed to causes, are always inclined to think that if a thing is proved to be an ideal it is proved to be the ideal. Many, for example, avowedly followed Cecil Rhodes because he had a vision. They might as well have followed him because he had a nose; a man without some kind of dream of perfection is quite as much of a monstrosity as a noseless man. People say of such a figure, in almost feverish whispers, "He knows his own mind," which is exactly like saying in equally feverish whispers, "He blows his own nose." Human nature simply cannot subsist without a hope and aim of some kind; as the sanity of the Old Testament truly said, where there is no vision the people perisheth. But it is precisely because an ideal is necessary to man that the man without ideals is in permanent danger of fanaticism. There is nothing which is so likely to leave a man open to the sudden and irresistible inroad of an unbalanced vision as the cultivation of business habits. All of us know angular business men who think that the earth is flat, or that Mr. Kruger was at the head of a great military despotism, or that men are graminivorous, or that Bacon wrote Shakespeare. Religious and philosophical beliefs are, indeed, as dangerous as fire, and nothing can take from them that beauty of danger. But there is only one way of really guarding ourselves against the excessive danger of them, and that is to be steeped in philosophy and soaked in religion.

Briefly, then, we dismiss the two opposite dangers of bigotry and fanaticism, bigotry which is a too great vagueness and fanaticism which is a too great concentration. We say that the cure for the bigot is belief; we say that the cure for the idealist is ideas. To know the best theories of existence and to choose the best from them (that is, to the best of our own strong conviction) appears to us the proper way to be neither bigot nor fanatic, but something more firm than a bigot and more terrible than a fanatic, a man with a definite opinion. But that definite opinion must in this view begin with the basic matters of human thought, and these must not be dismissed as irrelevant, as religion, for instance, is too often in our days dismissed as irrelevant. Even if we think religion insoluble, we cannot think it irrelevant. Even if we ourselves have no view of the ultimate verities, we must feel that wherever such a view exists in a man it must be more important than anything else in him. The instant that the thing ceases to be the unknowable, it becomes the indispensable. There can be no doubt, I think, that the idea does exist in our time that there is something narrow or irrelevant or even mean about attacking a man's religion, or arguing from it in matters of politics or ethics. There can be quite as little doubt that such an accusation of narrowness is itself almost grotesquely narrow. To take an example from comparatively current events: we all know that it was not uncommon for a man to be considered a scarecrow of bigotry and obscurantism because he distrusted the Japanese, or lamented the rise of the Japanese, on the ground that the Japanese were Pagans. Nobody would think that there was anything antiquated or fanatical about distrusting a people because of some difference between them and us in practice or political machinery. Nobody would think it bigoted to say of a people, "I distrust their influence because they are Protectionists." No one would think it narrow to say, "I lament their rise because they are Socialists, or Manchester Individualists, or strong believers in militarism and conscription." A difference of opinion about the nature of Parliaments matters very much; but a difference of opinion about the nature of sin does not matter at all. A difference of opinion about the object of taxation matters very much; but a difference of opinion about the object of human existence does not matter at all. We have a right to distrust a man who is in a different kind of municipality; but we have no right to mistrust a man who is in a different kind of cosmos. This sort of enlightenment is surely about the most unenlightened that it is possible to imagine. To recur to the phrase which I employed earlier, this is tantamount to saying that everything is important with the exception of everything. Religion is exactly the thing which cannot be left out —because it includes everything. The most absent-minded person cannot well pack his Gladstone-bag and leave out the bag. We have a general view of existence, whether we like it or not; it alters or, to speak more accurately, it creates and involves everything we say or do, whether we like it or not. If we regard the Cosmos as a dream, we regard the Fiscal Question as a dream. If we regard the Cosmos as a joke, we regard St. Paul's Cathedral as a joke. If everything is bad, then we must believe (if it be possible) that beer is bad; if everything be good, we are forced to the rather fantastic conclusion that scientific philanthropy is good. Every man in the street must hold a metaphysical system, and hold it firmly. The possibility is that he may have held it so firmly and so long as to have forgotten all about its existence.

This latter situation is certainly possible; in fact, it is the situation of the whole modern world. The modern world is filled with men who hold dogmas so strongly that they do not even know that they are dogmas. It may be said even that the modern world, as a corporate body, holds certain dogmas so strongly that it does not know that they are dogmas. It may be thought "dogmatic," for instance, in some circles accounted progressive, to assume the perfection or improvement of man in another world. But it is not thought "dogmatic" to assume the perfection or improvement of man in this world; though that idea of progress is quite as unproved as the idea of immortality, and from a rationalistic point of view quite as improbable. Progress happens to be one of our dogmas, and a dogma means a thing which is not thought dogmatic. Or, again, we see nothing "dogmatic" in the inspiring, but certainly most startling, theory of physical science, that we should collect facts for the sake of facts, even though they seem as useless as sticks and straws. This is a great and suggestive idea, and its utility may, if you will, be proving itself, but its utility is, in the abstract, quite as disputable as the utility of that calling on oracles or consulting shrines which is also said to prove itself. Thus, because we are not in a civilization which believes strongly in oracles or sacred places, we see the full frenzy of those who killed themselves to find the sepulchre of Christ. But being in a civilization which does believe in this dogma of fact for facts' sake, we do not see the full frenzy of those who kill themselves to find the North Pole. I am not speaking of a tenable ultimate utility which is true both of the Crusades and the polar explorations. I mean merely that we do see the superficial and aesthetic singularity, the startling quality, about the idea of men crossing a continent with armies to conquer the place where a man died. But we do not see the aesthetic singularity and startling quality of men dying in agonies to find a place where no man can live—a place only interesting because it is supposed to be the meeting-place of some lines that do not exist.

Let us, then, go upon a long journey and enter on a dreadful search. Let us, at least, dig and seek till we have discovered our own opinions. The dogmas we really hold are far more fantastic, and, perhaps, far more beautiful than we think. In the course of these essays I fear that I have spoken from time to time of rationalists and rationalism, and that in a disparaging sense. Being full of that kindliness which should come at the end of everything, even of a book, I apologize to the rationalists even for calling them rationalists. There are no rationalists. We all believe fairy-tales, and live in them. Some, with a sumptuous literary turn, believe in the existence of the lady clothed with the sun. Some, with a more rustic, elvish instinct, like Mr. McCabe, believe merely in the impossible sun itself. Some hold the undemonstrable dogma of the existence of God; some the equally undemonstrable dogma of the existence of the man next door.

Truths turn into dogmas the instant that they are disputed. Thus every man who utters a doubt defines a religion. And the scepticism of our time does not really destroy the beliefs, rather it creates them; gives them their limits and their plain and defiant shape. We who are Liberals once held Liberalism lightly as a truism. Now it has been disputed, and we hold it fiercely as a faith. We who believe in patriotism once thought patriotism to be reasonable, and thought little more about it. Now we know it to be unreasonable, and know it to be right. We who are Christians never knew the great philosophic common sense which inheres in that mystery until the anti-Christian writers pointed it out to us. The great march of mental destruction will go on. Everything will be denied. Everything will become a creed. It is a reasonable position to deny the stones in the street; it will be a religious dogma to assert them. It is a rational thesis that we are all in a dream; it will be a mystical sanity to say that we are all awake. Fires will be kindled to testify that two and two make four. Swords will be drawn to prove that leaves are green in summer. We shall be left defending, not only the incredible virtues and sanities of human life, but something more incredible still, this huge impossible universe which stares us in the face. We shall fight for visible prodigies as if they were invisible. We shall look on the impossible grass and the skies with a strange courage. We shall be of those who have seen and yet have believed.

THE END

Source

Heretics was copyrighted in 1905 by the John Lane Company. This electronic text is derived from the twelfth (1919) edition published by the John Lane Company of New York City and printed by the Plimpton Press of Norwood, Massachusetts. The text carefully follows that of the published edition (including British spelling).

Printed in Great Britain
by Amazon

37801020R00106